THEY CAME,
WE CONQUERED

THEY CAME, WE CONQUERED

Matt Rittenhouse

authorHOUSE®

AuthorHouse™ LLC
1663 Liberty Drive
Bloomington, IN 47403
www.authorhouse.com
Phone: 1-800-839-8640

Published by AuthorHouse   04/28/2014

ISBN: 978-1-4969-0926-8 (sc)
ISBN: 978-1-4969-0925-1 (e)

Table of Contents

Chapter 1:   The Sighting 1

Chapter 2:   Something Wrong...................................6

Chapter 3:   The Wait 24

Chapter 4:   The Hunt...49

Chapter 5:   The War.. 103

Chapter 6:   The Aftermath.................................... 160

About the Author.. 175

My name is Mic Von Haus. Where do I start, the weather I guess. It's been a well known fact since early 21st century or even late 20th century for that matter that greenhouse gasses affect global warming, and global warming throws weather patterns off. Now the most powerful tornadoes ever recorded; so strong and violent they rate beyond a category 5 rip through the Midwest, Texas and Oklahoma. Snow storms with sleet and ice can last nine or ten days, it can rain for two weeks straight. The summer solstice now starts on May 21 the fall solstice starts August 21, and so on. Floods occur and rivers get wider but people have long moved out of flooded areas. The roads have become so eroded it is impossible to keep up with construction repairs. The historic snow storm of 2129 where it snowed for a month straight, followed by the ultraviolent heat wave later that summer was a revolution for government spending. Now the design and mass production of flying cars is very well government funded. I was born in 2140 August 26th, my parents were amongst the first generation to learn how to operate flying cars. It was mandatory to learn everything from how they were started on the assembly line to what they are capable of to operate one. Eight weeks of two nights a week for two hours with a c or higher is what it takes. You must be 17 or a senior in high school to earn your certificate. The "Astro mobiles" have sensors that keep you five to seven feet above the eroded streets at speeds of 30 to 60 miles per hour. 60 to 200 miles per hour or "highway travel" move you to 50 to 100 feet above the ground. The slower you travel the closer to ground you stay. We still utilize the highway system because it's illegal to fly directly over any ones property. If you are caught cutting across for a shortcut it's a night in jail and your air mobile is impounded. The air mobile is very small and seats three people max, one driver and two in the back. People have become so self efficient and self dependant there's no need for room to take a bunch of belongings. And since the astro mobile is such an efficient way of travel there is no need for planes. The battery last long enough to make it across the Atlantic. 150 miles per hour is very typical for highway travel, you can push it to about 220 miles per hour but anything faster than that you're pushing your luck. Rural living has got rid of neighborhoods instead everyone lives in farming type communities. The average household has seven family members and owns at least an acre of land and grows a variety of vegetables. The inner cities have developed mega structures that house restaurants, retail stores, corporate offices and condos. The towers are massive 150 stories, three tier structures that are two blocks wide and two blocks deep. A top of the first two tiers there is room for a large park equipped with slides, a screened in movie projector and during the summer time plenty of room to toss a football or frisbee around. There's a large walking path like a warning track to the clear glass wall surrounding the whole park. And in the middle a tall free standing wall with water trickling down into a creek that spills into a concrete pond with assorted fresh water wildlife. On the outside are elevator systems operated with magnetic force. Chicago has one Milwaukee, Minneapolis, St. Paul, you get the picture; New York has two. They are connected to one and other with mega trams that are electric powered but depart and arrive with magnetic force. They are very fast and operate hundreds of feet above the ground at the center of each structure. This system was first put into place by the Chinese. An alluring profession is Hunter. Being able to track and kill your own food is a crucial skill to have these days. Almost everyone hunts or at least fish, but to be very good at hunting a variety of wild life can make you a lot of money. Medicine has drastically changed, too many medications with major side effects occurred during a surge of pharmaceutical companies who thought they all had a miracle drug that cured cancer and this miracle medicine went into just about everything from cough medicine to diabetic treatments. Now you don't take cough or cold medicine, it's banned. Antibiotics are the only medicine that circulates through the sick and diseased population. Prescriptions for sleeplessness and restless leg syndrome and others like that are banned. Plus the only form of pain killer is morphine so you must be in very intense pain or dying to get that. Politicians have changed. The change was forced from an up rise in Washington D.C when thousands of people took to the streets to protest against privacy laws and far too much government control. When the cops tried shutting them down the angry mobs got violent, a lot of civilians lost their lives as well as many officers. That sprung about not only a reconstruction of government policies but a new line of law enforcement came about. Today the officers are equipped with infantry training, and are not concerned with petty crimes. It's great because no one goes around sticking their nose in every ones business. I became an officer and work six hour shifts. It's become standard to only work six hour at a time no one gets burned out. Factories and hospitals acquired another shift. I don't like the city life I prefer my ranch in the country. I garden, I have a few tomato plants, just over a quarter acre of corn stalks, and I grow green beans, and carrots. I have a peach tree as well. I keep a cow on my property that mates with my neighbor's bull and once the calf grows up I split the meat with them. I keep half a dozen chickens on my land as well, I love fresh eggs. My neighbors who have three children two girls and a boy share a well with me. No one wants to rely on grocery stores anymore. My days are pretty laid back for the most part. I start off with some exercise then around mid morning start my patrol. Then take care of my chores and finish my evenings spending quality time with my family. I have three kids of my own, three girls. I constantly keep up with my rifle and bow and arrow skills. I'm like Robin Hood with my bow and arrow and can put a bullet in the head of my enemies from nine-hundred yards with my M110 sniper rifle. I take my rifle and my Berretta 9mm along with me on my patrol. I was on patrol the day the visitors came.

Chapter 1

THE SIGHTING

Mic was out in the open country side investigating an abandoned animal trap with the carcass of a deer stuck in it. He could see two little boys in the distance coming towards him. He tucked his buck knife away and waited on a nearby hickory log for them to reach him.

"What's new boys?"

"Did you hear about the new people officer?"

"What new people?"

"I don't know, no one has seen them before. They're really big." The boys pause for a second.

"there's three of them in a field north of interstate 80."

Mic thinks for a second. "Three of them." He states puzzled. From the way the boys sounded excited he figured they meant something out of the ordinary was going on.

"Three really tall people?"

"No these weren't people." Replied the boys. "We don't know who they are."

"Who else saw them?"

"Just us and the people living on the property."

"What were they doing?"

"Just standing there then you couldn't see them anymore."

Mic said; "You guys better go straight home."

"Yes sir." Said the boys. They all headed in the same direction before they parted separate ways Mic asked; "How far along 80 were they?" They answered,

"two or three more miles east at the house on the right."

"Ok."

Mic headed to the house where the visitors were spotted it appeared as no one was home so Mic went to the front door and rang the door bell. The family was monitoring the perimeter from their crawl space and came out to greet him. Mic collected the same info from them as he did from the boys. The family mentioned they saw Mic go bye on his patrol about a half-hour earlier and saw the boys out and about and told them to go find him then ran into their crawl space. Having no more information on them Mic decided to carry on his way home. He hurried home fearful that there were more of them around his property, and since he had not seen them he did not know what to expect. He tried to contact his family using his radio, there was no response. He tried not to panic they could be out gardening he thought. He couldn't wait any longer he tried radioing them again, still no response. He quickened his pace. He tried a third time still no response. He went to a full sprint and when he got within a mile of his house tried again and his wife Debra answered "Yes."

"Is everything alright ?" Mic said with a panic.

"Yes is something wrong?" asked Debra. Mic slowed down to a light jog. He wasn't sure how to answer so he said, "I'll tell you when I get home I'm almost home." When he walked in he hurried to the sink for a glass of water, he leaned against the counter and asked Debra to gather the kids. Once everyone was around he sat his water down and told them;

"Debra, Erica, Stacy, Jasmine, there are some unusual people around we need to keep our eyes peeled for them. If they come around here we know what to do, right."

"Yes Daddy."

Mic looked at his wife she gave a firm nod yes. "Ok" said Mic. The girls went back to playing in the yard. Mic fallowed Debra back to their tomato plants, he informed her what the family and two young boys saw. She agreed it was unusual and was glad everyone was safe but still longed for Mic to remain at the house. Mic was always humble and never to proud for the concern of his family and agreed to call an end to his patrol and keep a look out for his home and family.

Chapter Two

Something Wrong

The next morning after some exercise he heard his neighbor Ray calling on the radio. "Mic, can you help me with something?" Mic answered on the radio,

"What do you need Ray?"

"It's easier to show you." Said Ray.

"Ok I'll be right over." Replied Mic. Mic headed over to his neighbors house. He walked up to the front door; Ray saw him coming and opened it just before reached the top step.

"Come in." Said Ray.

"What do you need help with?" Ray turned and walked to his kitchen table, he motioned for Mic to sit down.

"What I'm about to tell is hard to understand I mean it's easy to understand it's hard to comprehend." Mic thought for a moment.

"Why don't you just show me?"

"Alright." Ray takes a deep breath before he gets up. He heads to his back yard, Mic fallows him. What he sees as he walks through the yard shocks Mic.

"How is this possible?"

Ray does not say anything the look on his face says it all. A loud jet engine sound crept closer "What happened?" Mic shouted.

"There wasn't this much last time I was out here." Shouted Ray

"Is that blood?" the jet engine was very loud now it sounded like it was right above them. The two of them looked up at the same time only to find they could not see anything. Then a loud boom and fireball blast burst through the sky. It appeared as something shot through the sky at an incredible rate they tried to locate where the sound went and where the fireball came from, puzzled they both headed back to the house. "That was blood on your lawn wasn't it." Mic stated.

"Yes from our bull, there wasn't that much before I called you. The girls discovered it on their way to the corn field, they ran in got me and I called you, but there's more now."

Just then Mic noticed out Ray's window his chickens were wondering over, they were approaching the blood pool in a scattered line and one at a time as they reached the edge they burst and evaporated leaving a fresh layer of blood on the ground. Actually seeing it made both men very nervous about even stepping foot outside. Mic rushed to Ray's radio.

"Debra! Come in Debra! Don't go outside don't let anyone go outside!" a few seconds go by.

Then Debra shouts over the radio "Jasmine is outside!"

Mic drops the radio runs out Ray's back door threw the field and sees Jasmine about to get on the swing. Worried something could happen when she sits down Mic yells "Hey don't sit down." Jasmine stops looks at her father, "What" Mic shouts, "run inside, NOW!" so she turns and runs as fast as she can into they're house. Mic runs in behind her. "Some real freaky shhh" remembering not to swear in front of jasmine, corrects himself "junk, out there." He catches his breath. "our chickens are gone, dead!"

"How, what happened?"

"I don't know there is like a force field out there that exploded Norman, Rays Bull, then like the chickens were possessed to see what happened wandered into it and they exploded."

"What?" Said Debra.

"I saw them coming across the yard not making sound, like zombies fallowing one after the other to a particular spot then suddenly exploding and evaporating." "Exploding then evaporating?" "Yes first bursting to pieces then in mid air the pieces just evaporate."

"What was that big boom?"

"I don't know, it sounded like a jet was right above us but we couldn't see anything then the loud boom, and a fireball blast, and it sounded like the craft or jet sped off." He expresses with great enthusiasm. "We need to deal with that force field or whatever . . ." he states directly but calmly. "Get armed with your weapon, Stacy with hers, Erica with hers."

Mic runs to the gun cabinet in the hallway; he grabs the M110 sniper rifle locks down the ammo, chow slings it, grabs his berretta 9mm, then his M16 lock and loads that; and while Debra frantically grabs hers and the kids hand guns. He slides his buck knife into its holster and onto his belt buckle, he yells down the hall to Debra, "Wait for my signal on the radio to come over to Ray's alright."

"Yes honey." she replies; she runs into Erica's room where all the girls are huddled and double checks the safety feature individually before handing them out and incase they didn't get the picture reminds them "Safeties on push it the other way before firing." They gather around the bedroom window to see if they can see what they're husband and father are doing. They see a baseball get hurled in the air, and then they're husband and father running after it, then chucking it again and again running after it, the girls look real confused. Then by the third throw Debra is reminded of the force field and is no longer left puzzled. A few moments later Mic radios in that he has made it to Ray's house and to take a direct path here in a straight line. Once all accounted for Mic and Ray stand on his deck, Ray armed with a semiautomatic 12 gage they were discussing what they know and what they don't know about the force field.

"We know one side starts their;" using his rifle to point; "because we saw my chickens walk right into it."

"I got a feeling it expands past the pool of blood, my bull must have been walking that way."

"Get me some more balls, a tennis ball and football."
Ray goes to his garage and comes back with a tennis
ball, football, soccer ball and a frisbee.

"I'm going to go out and through these one at a time
till we get an idea of how wide it is."

"Ok good."

Mic walks out a little way, heaves the baseball, it
incinerates, then aims further left with the football,
it incinerates, then further with the frisbee, it to
incinerates, then with the tennis ball, it lands clear in
the field.

"Ok now we have an idea . . ." Just as he's about to
finish some other animals come wandering in the yard.
Making no noise the neighbor's ducks and chicken walk
in, burst into pieces and evaporate. Looking at each
other they have two separate things on their mind, Ray
lets Mic talk first.

"From where they were at we know how wide it is,
we have two of four sides found."

Ray nods. "Yes, something is drawing the animals in." He proclaims. "Do you see anything or smell anything; that would draw them in."

Mic shakes his head. "It's weird." They both head inside to collaborate. "I think its best we avoid it till now. "We need to find out how deep it is." adding, "how far back it goes and how high."

"Everyone go to the living room." Ray says to his family and Mic's family fallows.

"These must be set by the other people."

"The force field?" Asks Ray.

"Yea."

"What other people?"

"A family and a couple of boys saw some strange people yesterday. A family a few miles east down interstate 80. I thought you would have heard about them by now."

"No were you on patrol?"

"Yea. Like an hour after I started these two boys came up to me and told me about them."

"Did you see them?"

"No."

"What did they look like?"

"I didn't see them; the boys said they were really big."

"Who are they?"

"I don't know. I think they're aliens." Mic says in a whisper trying not to let anyone else hear. Ray looks very surprised.

"Let's listen to the news." Ray dials his radio to the news station. Mic turns the monitor to the media network.

"Maybe the media has said something about all this." The media is now one very large corporation. The internet and television has integrated and one media channel keeps you updated with all sports, daily, and weather news twenty-four, seven with different anchors every six hours. When he first walked over to the big monitor in the wall and turned it on by waving his hand over the bottom right corner a thirty

14

second advertisement was playing. The radio wasn't broadcasting an emergency alert and when the news came back the anchor, who is a very stunning brunet, with gorgeous eyes, and voluptuous lips and favors sports news was saying;

"I'm Ashly Walker for Greener Globe Media. Last night's game 6 of the NBA finals was a thriller at the coliseum, Gulf Coast Sea Port Arena was sold out with just over 200,000 in attendance, Miami, Heat pulled off a close one against the Los Angeles, Lakers. Miami's leading shot blocker Arian Jackson had 5 rejections . . . this just in something unusual is stirring threw the mid-west, in Iowa, Nebraska, and Kansas reports of force fields attracting and incinerating animals and livestock, graphic footage depicts what is happening." The network roles the footage leaving Ashly's reaction on display. Obviously horrified she tries her best to remain professional.

"The force fields are 30 yards by 50 yards, and that is all the information we currently have on them. As we gather more info on them we will keep you informed. Uh I'm just getting now that there are twenty or more force fields scattered through Iowa, Nebraska, and Kansas. Joining us now over the radio is Dr. Afton O'neal head of NASA's space monitoring team, Dr. O'neal share with us your knowledge on the force fields."

"Yes, as you are aware we monitor every corner of the Milky Way Galaxy and far beyond, and did not see anything carrying alien life form. And everyone is aware of the alien sightings across America, so they got hear undetected. And that is a scary thought."

Ashly blurts out; "13 states reported so far, including California, Idaho, Washington, Montana, North Dakota, South Dakota, Kansas, Nebraska, Iowa, Kentucky, Tennessee, Arkansas, Maryland, North Carolina, and South Carolina, so 15 states. Sorry to interrupt please proceed with your analysis."

"Yes, I don't intend to put fear into anyone but every American citizen should be alarmed. Our early speculation is that the force fields are an attempt to weaken us by taking away one of our primary nutrition sources which of course would be our livestock. If a battle for our planet were to rage on destroying our various resources for food would be the first chess move. And we don't know enough about our visitors or they're force fields to attack right now, the best thing is we urge everyone to get to their safest hiding spot and stay there."

"Yes getting to a safe hiding quickly and quietly is your best bet right now." Ashly states.

Then the emergency alert is sounded over the radio, you can hear in the background as everyone gets more and more captivated by the news report.

"We have many questions about the force fields and we have secretary of Stratus Defense Dr. Berry Rosenbaum here via satellite to answer them. Good morning; or afternoon where you're at Dr. Rosenbaum."

"Yes, good morning to you Ashly."

"Dr. Rosenbaum, what can you tell us about the force fields?"

"Yes, a force of this magnitude would run out of power eventually, but given the advance mechanism of it there's no telling that they may have an unlimited power supply. But we can rule out solar because to our knowledge they have been working since before the sun came up. There must be a disarming code that either the aliens carry on them or from they're space craft's we can't locate. Just stay calm and keep guard we will inform you as we find out more. Thank you."

"Thanks Dr. Rosenbaum. We will continue with other news but as events unfold we will keep you informed."

Keeping calm is easier these days. Long ago looting and robbing were proven a failure since everyone's house is so far apart and every rancher is heavily armed.

As everyone tries to draw their attention away from the monitor Mic says; "we will all stay together hear, girls keep your arms and head to the crawl space. Jeff stay with your father and I, we will keep an eye on the force field. Jeff gets an overwhelming sense of duty, honor, and courage as he cocks his M16 and heads out to the deck with his dad and Mic. Mic heads back in and grabs two more portable radios. They all listen as they watch and try to figure out a counter approach.

"I know we talk about this from time to time but I want to make sure your girls know what to do in this situation?"

"Of course." Replies Ray. Mic nods. They are all silent for a moment, then Jeff breaks the silence by saying;

"I can put a bullet in the head of those things ten times out of ten from 400 yards with my M16."

"I could do that from 600 yards."

"Really?"

"I'm Marksman with my M110 rifle, I can do ten head shots out of ten from 990 yards. Just over 900 meters.

"That's what that badge on your arm represents?"

"Yes it does . . . your dad can go what ten out of ten from 55yards with his 9mm."

"Maybe eight or nine out ten from there, probably one miss and one throat or chest hit."

"How did you get real good dad?" After slinging his 12 gage semi automatic over his shoulder he replies;

"Lots of target practice, and lots of firing drills with Mic."

"I wander what they look like." Jeff says.

"I have heard one description, they're tall and big."

"What do you think they're doing here?"

"I don't know." Answers his father.

"Do you think we will have to kill some of them?"

His father hesitates for a second, then says; "Maybe, if the situations calls for it." Mic agrees with a head nod. Then Ray notices . . .

Mic Yell, "Hey Betsy, HEY!" Ray instinctively grips his shotgun firmly. Mic runs past them and runs up to Betsy. Panic creeps up on them; they don't know what to do, simultaneously they shout,

"Mic!"

Mic gets close to Betsy, he yells at her to get away. She keeps going closer. He tugs at her collar. She puts up a fight and keeps moving on. He gives another tug letting out a grunt and yells,

"BETSY!" He lets go and pulls out his Berretta 9mm and shoots her in the head. It's silent for a second.

"I wasn't going to let the Aliens kill her." Mic hollers.

Jeff and Ray head to the garage and come back with a tarp, they head across to Mic and together they slide her on and pull her to the house. After just witnessing Mic's display of professional execution out of desperation made Jeff very eager to kill an alien. Ray says;

"I'll butcher her for you, and put her in the freezer."

"Thanks, take the usual." Mic says; "I haven't used a bullet to kill something in five years."

He starts reminiscing about the last time he killed someone.

"You remember the Ranger Officers in Detroit that were real pissed off and fed up? Marine Force Recon

Bravo Company 249 got called up for duty, and our platoons were large squad teams. There were six squads of 20 men and I was leader of squad three. We did a precision parachute jump 4 miles south of Detroit we ran into the city; we briefly stopped three quarter miles short of the city for equipment check and a M.O briefing. I commanded positions and where to rendezvous for mission status. It was Rangers and Infantry officers, they started off protesting only for a couple of days; then they were rioting and the civilians defended themselves with pretty heavy arms. The number of killed climbed drastically. We needed to neutralize power by killing the highly trained, heavily armed officers and detain or even capture as many civilians as we could. We killed and arrested many officers and unfortunately had to kill many civilians who were desperately seeking revenge. After knocking off the officers it was door to door raids confiscating weapons without licenses and arresting and trying those witnessed doing violent crimes during that time. We spent four weeks neutralizing the area and another four weeks staying guard. It was something that divided everyone in that area. But this is something we'll all pull together through."

"Amen to that." Ray and Jeff say at the same time. After full participation butchering the cow, spending the afternoon and evening closely together and closely on watch the two families were trying to relax playing card games and family games. The news didn't have much more to communicate. Since it was hard to be at ease, Mic suggested a slumber party in the Dawson's crawl space, they will watch movies and have snacks and see what the next day brings.

Chapter 3

THE WAIT

We have waited for two weeks now. We still don't know how to deal with the force fields. Periodically livestock and game would wander into the force field, but that hasn't happened for six days. We listen in on the radio for clues to why the visitors are here, and what's their motive. No humans have been attacked yet, but they have greatly increased in numbers. It makes it hard to keep calm knowing the minimum. Everyone is doing a great job. I'm impressed with how well everyone is holding up and staying rational. We all go up as a unit. My family and I head to our house for showers and they stay at theirs. Then either they come over for the night or we go back over to their crawl space. We have not seen any Aliens on our property yet. We have seen plenty of images and clips of them on the monitors; they are huge, with tails that come down to a flat spear head. Any images you see are only for a few seconds because they have special camouflage skin that changes any different color of a background so they become practically invisible. I believe along with many others they're waiting for us to have to go out and hunt, then they hunt us. One thing I don't think they counted on is now mostly everyone has a year supply of food stored. It will be quite the waiting game. If they get impatient and come into our homes they will be at a huge disadvantage. So we will wait, and keep our faith and spirits up.

After a hot soup and grilled cheese lunch Mic and Jasmine are huddled in a cozy corner Jasmine on her dads lap sets up a game of solitaire on the floor, before she starts to play she sighs and says; "How long have you been a special agent officer daddy?"

"Oh seven years now sweetie."

"Is that a long time?"

"Well its one less year than you have been alive, so it's only been a short time in that sense."

"Will you protect us from the monsters daddy?"

"Of course, I will protect you from anything."

Then Stacy comes over and asks; "What did you do before National Security?"

"Before I became a special agent I joined the Marines after your mother and I got married. My first job was infantry for two years, then your mom was pregnant with Erica, so I became Marine Recon.

"Why Recon dad, is that better?"

"It is, I wanted Recon because it was more training and more training means more skills, and increases my chance for survival."

"Could you survive eight tornadoes, no ten tornadoes, and a giant blizzard?"

"Well ten tornadoes would be very powerful I would get sucked away, and trapped between all of them, I would be like AAWWWWW!" He pretends convulsing like he's stuck in a twirly trap. "Luckily ten is not likely, two or three could happen. And I would know much better than most people what to do."

"What about a tornado and a blizzard?" Jasmine wanders.

"I would wrap you guys in lots of blankets and hold on to you guys as tight as I could so the tornado doesn't suck you away."

"We would be blowing in the air and you would be holding on to the blankets." Says Stacy.

"You mean I would watch you guys blow away and just stand there holding the blankets?"

The girls laugh. "No dad, we would be in the blankets about to fly away but you would be holding on pulling us in." Stacy says with a smile.

"You mean like this." He picks them up one at a time over his head and spins them around. After playing they notice it starts to rain again, they can hear it hitting the ground above them. Jasmine in a whimper says;

"I hate the rain this is the 1000 day it's rained."

"It has only been five days." Stacy declares.

"We've had four whole days of sun since we went into hiding." Moans Jasmine.

"What do you want to do?" Momma asks sounding stern. "Play your solitaire you set up."

"I've played like 500 times."

"Then clean it up." Momma demands.

A few more days pass, so not to risk a careless death the two families feel it's wise not running back and forth anymore and bunk up at their own shacks. Mic and his family hang out upstairs and keep the noise to a minimum to not attract attention. Mic keeps close guard on his family. He and Debra see to it that every night the girls are read to and maintain a hygienic routine. Mic sleeps when he can, but worry about his daughters and beautiful wife keep him a wake most of the time. Right after the sun goes down they all hunker in their crawl space. It didn't get much use before, but it is an excellent safe hide out. They are surrounded by three feet thick steel walls. It is equipped with all the amenities the house has except for a fire place. Its air conditioned and has a basic ventilation system blended with their home. The door to get in is virtually invisible. In the basement the back wall has a painting hanging at head level, it's actually the latch. The far end has an escape hatch that is impossible to see from above, and can only be opened from the inside. Although the crawl space has running water they keep a two year supply of bottled water in the pantry. They have plenty of food in the fridge and the huge walk in freezer is stocked with sealed veggies from their land.

"How long do we have to stay inside?" asks Erica.

"However long it takes to figure out how to rid the aliens." Answers her father. "I don't think they planned on us having a two year supply of food. Maybe they will figure that out and leave, at least our area. Is there anything good on Debra?"

"I'm watching the news."

"Let's watch something else."

They thumb through the various sitcoms till they find one they all agree on.

"I like this show." Says Stacy.

"Is this your favorite show?" Asks momma.

"Yea, one of my favorites. I like Muppets VS Mouppets and Space Rangers."

"What about The Worker?"

"Oh I love the The Worker! It's funny."

"How about you Jasmine?"

"I like The Sanctuary Fairies."

"Yea that's a very good show. What's your favorite show Erica?"

"The Worker and The Boys Are Back."

"Mines The Worker what's yours darling?"

"Mine are The Housing Project, and The Worker."

"I thought you were going to say you like watching football the best." States Stacy.

"Oh yea." Replies Mic then lounges out of his spot on the couch, he picks up Stacy and tackles her. And Says, "Your caught in the daddy love trap." Jasmine laughing piles on top of her daddy, Erica and Debra laugh while maintaining their spots on the couch.

"I know," Momma says; "let's do a Tic Tac Tow tournament."

After a long grueling tournament they all settle down in the bedroom and call it a night. Another night safely in the books. As the months go by it gets colder and colder. A blizzard came, for six straight days it snowed. During that time it was so dark you couldn't tell night from day. From lack of sleep Mic would sometimes nap for hours not knowing if it were am or pm when he woke up. It would be getting warmer soon, but their meat supply was running out.

"This is the last of Betsy." Said Mic.

Having a good sense of hummer has tremendous value being stuck inside. At the dinner table Mic continues with his crude positive attitude; "Can you pass more Betsy please?" instead of conserving Betsy Mic goes all out with the last steak and hamburger feast that would make past time kings and queens jealous. "Umm Betsy is delicious." Sensing everyone is getting a sad uneasy feeling Mic says; "We should be serious about this and since we have not said grace in a long time I will say grace. Everyone close your eyes. Dear Lord thank you . . ." a big boom shakes the table. "Huh, oh my god what was that?" Another boom, but he was busted they saw him whack the bottom of the table.

"Dad!" The girls say simultaneously.

"Ha ha got ya. Ok, ok close your eyes." Mimicking a Hymn he goes; "Awwwawawaw, Awwwawawaw" the girls giggle and mom gives a stern look. Mic clears his throat and starts again; "Lord thank you for Betsy I'm glad we didn't let those damn dirty aliens get their long webbed fingers on our beloved cow, she taste great. Amen." After a few more weeks go by Mic knows it will be up to him to go on a hunt and get more food. The girls have no problem going vegetarian but Mic is not only craving more meat but for his sanity he needs to get out and do something for himself. He inspects his M110 barrel, loads it, packs his knife and compass, and straps on his 9mm and informs his wife he will be back shortly. She begs him to stay stating,

"It will be worm again in a couple or a few weeks."

"Yea but the aliens will still be here and their F ing force fields I'm not only hunting game I'm going to kill the aliens too."

"No you don't know that there could be more force fields we don't know about."

"That's not likely and I . . ."

"Plus no animals have been around for months."

"I will head straight north for about 20 miles." He gestures at his compass. "We know there aren't any in that direction for at least 30-40 miles. I will have my sharpest wits about me, I promise."

"You could walk right into one and not know it."

"If I take this a long I will be fine." Mic walks over to his gun and ammo supply cabinet and grabs his stringed tennis ball. "It will take some time but I will be as careful as a girl in new shoes surrounded by mud." That doesn't put Debra's mind at ease but it will have to do because she knows once her hubby has his mind set on something there's no changing it. He gives Debra a long sensual kiss goodbye, the girls' line up to tell their papa goodbye. Sobbing one at a time they wish their daddy good luck on his hunt and leave him with a sweet smooch on his check. Bundled up and hunting equipped he scans the perimeter before heading into the grey. Once he gets a few miles down range he swings his tennis ball in a circular motion out in front of him. He had practiced this technique for many hours as he had nothing else to do. He practiced and practiced knowing this time would come. He gets a few more miles before he notices a sign the aliens are in the area; foot prints in the snow. He tucks his tennis ball and string away and gets his M110 at the low ready. He crouches down and scans which direction to fallow. Before he trails the foot prints he rubs one with his fingers and smells it the scent isn't strong so he knows he has a way to go to catch up to them. He quickens his pace to a steady jog. He meets up with more foot prints; he knows there will be three of them. Hot on their trail his adrenaline boosts him to a full out sprint. He keeps it up for a great distance, hurdling logs and brushing threw branches; he's closing in on them. Then he suddenly comes to a stop. He sniffs the air, he knows they are very close. Checking all directions, he does not see them. He braces himself against a tree thinking of what to do next. He starts to dig a fox hole. Clearing the snow he breaks through the ground, half way through he senses something, then he hears something behind him, he whips around . . . there's nothing he puts down his shovel and grabs his knife, he knows it will be close combat. He remembers they can camouflage themselves with anything, he tunnels his vision between two trees, he spots the alien. Knowing he has been spotted the alien shows his true skin color and walks aggressively towards Mic. For the first time he is face to face with the alien, he is massive, over seven feet tall with a long spear like tail. With the alien bearing down on him he re-grips his knife. Closer and closer the alien gets and lets out a loud growling yell but Mic is ready he lounges at the alien with his knife. With one swift move the alien dodges it and swings his spear head tail at Mic hitting him in the chest and knocking him down. Rolling to his feet he takes out his 9mm, before he turns off the safety; with his tail the alien knocks it out of his hand. Back to his original approach. Keeping himself square with the alien as it circles around him he jabs at it with his knife he hits only the air that's ok though he's only trying to keep him distanced. With its massive reach the alien swipes at Mic's head, he ducks it, the razor sharp claws at the end of the aliens webbed fingers come within an inch of Mic's face. Mic could feel the trailing wind produced from the swipe. The alien thrashes his tail at him. He jumps back. Then the other two aliens appear in his peripheral vision, but he does not want to take his eyes off his current opponent. The alien hisses at him revealing a gruesome set of long razor sharp teeth. With the other two stalking in closer he knows he needs to finish this quickly. He runs towards a fallen tree, using the tree as leverage he steps then leaps in the air, twisting to the alien; he plunges his knife into its cheek and quickly let's go falling to the ground to dodge another tail thrash. Spinning to his knees with a sweeping motion he trips the alien, it crashes to ground. He quickly mounds the alien with his left knee over the alien's throat and his right foot planted on the ground, he rips out his knife from its check and forcefully drives into the aliens head. His gun is too far out of reach but he is fully confident now so it does not matter he knows being undersized has its advantage as well. He knows his quickness can't be matched by the fierce predators. However he lost sight of the other two. He keeps his head on a swivel scanning where he last saw them. Then he catches a glimpse of one to his right running towards him. He tries to locate it. For a second he losses it in the shadows, he backs up to a lighter spot and sees it right in front him. He quickly lunges at it sticking him in the stomach with his blade. With purple blood flowing from the wound it barely fazes the alien. It backhands Mic. The blow to his ear knocks him off balance and he falls to his butt. He quickly springs to a squatting position dodging another gusty swipe. The momentum brings the alien another step closer to Mic and he thrusts his knife into the aliens belly as he gets into his ready stance. This one penetrates deeper then the first. Now the alien is hesitant and tries to counter with his tail but Mic slashes it. The force of the knife meeting the end of his tail removes it from his body. Now badly injured the alien staggers at Mic, taking a wild swipe at him but Mic uses his knife to block it cutting off most of his hand leaving just his thumb and half his palm. He will be easy to finish now. But Mic gets a disturbing surprise he can feel the third alien right behind him. He ducks this alien's swipe just in time for it to perforate his buddy's face. Mic hurriedly changes direction the alien fallows. In the background the alien falls face down to the ground. Angry the alien charges at Mic. Mic backs up, it keeps coming after him. Mic falls back with the alien throwing himself on top of Mic, he gets a hold of the aliens wrist with one hand and bats off his claws with his knife. Taking multiple stabs to the hand the alien repeatedly tries to impale Mic's face. Laying there he knows he needs to do something quick. So he throws down his knife and catches the alien's wrist stopping his claws inches from his eyes. He pulls his arms apart and head butts the alien right in his chin stunning the alien. Mic keeps himself out of the aliens reach by wrapping his legs around his shoulder and head. With all his might he busts free from the hold so forcefully it flips Mic face down. He jumps to his feet noticing his gun lying on the ground, without hesitation he runs as fast as he can to it, dives for it, rolls on his back and unloads three to its chest one to its throat and one to its head. Surrounded by a pool of blood the alien lies there motionless, Mic stands over it and puts one more in its head just to be safe. He goes over to the dismembered tail and examines it for a minute. He decides to take it with him because if nothing else he can kill one of those sons of bitches with a severed tail. A little warn out he walks his trail back to his house very satisfied that he will settle for just veggies until all the aliens have been killed. It is late when he returns back home Debra and the kids have anxiously awaited his return they embrace him with many hugs. "Well I did not get anything for supper." He proclaims.

"That is ok papa." Say the girls

"What happened?" asks Debra as she notices the abrasion on the side of his head. He pulls out the alien tail from his satchel.

"I killed three of those bastards."

"You did? Way to go papa!" The girls say very enthused.

"Way to go hubby!"

As the night settles down they gather around their hubby and father in the living room as he shares his brutal victory with them.

"Tonight we can sleep in our regular bedrooms."

"You think so dad?" Stacy asks. He hesitates for a moment soaking in the anticipation.

"Yea I think its safe enough."

"If aliens come by here dad will protect us." Says Erica.

"Dad will kill them!" Says Jasmine.

"Oh yea, I miss our bed." Says Debra.

They play they're favorite card games, get into their pajamas and scurry to bed. Mic lays his M16 on the floor next to the bed and his 9mm on the night stand. Debra and Mic have some romantic time in the bedroom before hitting the lights. After they watch a little television they dim the lights put on some music, light a couple of candles and massage each other. Mic starts with Debra. He massages her neck then her shoulders and then her lower back. He finishes with her calves before doing her front. He sits next to her and massages her temples. Afterward kisses her on the forehead and gently caresses every delicate inch of her body. He gently glides his fingers up and down her arms, her hands, and down her fingers. He brushes his fingers against her body, along her sides, and down her hips. Then completes the treatment by massaging her ankles, feet and toes. She returns the favor by starting the same treatment but by the time she gets to his lower back he is sound asleep. She kisses her king on the cheek and joins him in bed. Over the next few days the family enjoys some moments outdoors together, still remaining cautious they carry their weapons at all times. After completing some chores they check the news on the monitors for any developing theories. Ashly Walker is pleased to report that three Navy SEAL teams captured over 300 of them in Wisconsin.

"At last some progress." Mic says hastily.

"What happened?" Asks Debra

"Three Navy SEAL teams caught 300 aliens in Wisconsin."

"What are they going to do with them?"

"It sounds like keep them captive in a prison outside Washington D.C. Maybe they will study them. Hear lets listen."

He waves his hand over the volume control on the monitor to turn it up. They can hear Ashly report;

"You may have just heard that 300 plus aliens were captured and transferred to a penitentiary outside Washington D.C. The name of the prison holding the aliens is Maryland House of Corrections Annex. It is an old prison that has not been used for decades. There, a strategic team of scientist, doctors and interrogation specialist as well as communication specialist will observe and try to learn as much as they can about the aliens. We will keep you informed as details develop."

"Wow that's incredible." Debra says.

"You can say that again." Mic replies.

During they're confinement for over two weeks they were studied and observed for countless hours trying to figure out how to communicate with them. After repeated failed attempts the interrogation became violent, the aliens were beaten and threatened with death, and still got nowhere. Finally as a last resort due to vague results and the privacy invasion act the aliens were sedated and hooked up to nuero imaging transmitters. They're thoughts and memories were displayed on monitors. Those images were studied and decoded. Also a communication breakthrough, one alien tired of being beaten, telepathically sent images to the militant man interrogating him, sharing what he thinks will happen to us. Between the two breakthroughs it was concluded they are terrorist groups from planet Acacia looking to terrorize and conquer our planet. Many questions were asked about the force fields and another communication breakthrough came about. They understood what we were asking them and they displayed the answers on the nuero imaging transition monitors. They revealed that a way to relinquish they're force field powers is by utilizing a disarming code from inside they're space craft's. So now a hunt for their space ships is about to begin knowing very well they will be hunting us.

At dinner every ones mood has been dampened because even though they knew Mic would be called in for duty it's very dreadful not being with their papa. Mic loves doing what he does for the daily adventure but he equally dreads being away from his family. They're all he thinks about whenever he's in a hostile environment for months at a time. That's all he needs as extra motivation to constantly keep his head on right and always alert and focused on making it home alive. It helps him always know what to do next. He knows how much they love him. After dinner it will be difficult to tell his girls that he and his company will be stationed in the most hostile area on the planet to find the aliens space ships, a place where for the past couple week's man and alien have been battling. It is best to tell the truth instead lie and say he will be back in a couple of weeks.

"Do you girls want to do something special tonight?"

"Yea." Answers Erica.

"What should we do?" Asks Jasmine.

"Let's watch all our favorite movies and say who is which character."

Mic decides not to spoil the movies and waits till they are over to tell them.

"Girls, Deb, I have something important to tell you. Tomorrow I ship out to Goodfellow Air Force Base in San Angelo Texas. I will be gone a long time. Probably nine months to a year, but I will return as fast and as safe as I can, as always." The girls sob, particularly Jasmine and Stacy. Jasmine runs into her room and throws herself on her bed and cry's into her pillow. Erica slowly walks to her bedroom with tears in her eyes. Stacy wraps her arms around her daddy's waist and soaks his shirt with tears. He does an extra good job tucking them all in, and tells them to be strong and look after momma. He walks down the hall Deb is waiting for him.

"What about here wont anyone be here to defend us from the aliens?" Asks Deb.

"A National Guard infantry unit will be assigned here to hunt and fight the aliens. They are sending the elite special agent companies to the most hostile areas, I'm hoping we can rid all the force fields in that area fast and then help rid the aliens from here if not already taken care of." He looks at her for a moment. "It will be ground combat, relinquishing the force fields of their power is our objective then we will see how things play out from there." He stares at her again. "God I love you sweetie." He kisses her forehead. Deb gets the overwhelming urge to seduce him. She quickly pulls his shirt over his head and kisses his chest. He lets out a passionate sigh. He then moves her back and rips open her shirt. They go to passionate kissing. She kisses him lower on the neck, then even lower on his chest again. He lets out another moan. She glides her fingers down his belly. She pulls open his pants and slides them down. With her fingers in his waistband she presses her open mouth against his inner thigh, she touches her tongue to his leg and wiggles it back and forth slowly. Mic says;

"Oh" in a quiet whisper. She moves her hands around his waistband and firmly grabs his butt. He can barely contain himself. He lifts her to her feet then throws her over his shoulder. He steadies her by forcefully grabbing her thick ass hard. He lays her on the bed and they make passionate love behind closed doors.

Chapter 4

THE HUNT

On the plane ride to Goodfellow Air Force Base some of the younger less experienced privates looked nervous. I remember thinking to myself it's ok to be nervous sometimes it helps you think faster, however sometimes it makes you freeze up and that's how you get killed. The M.Plane or Military Plane arrived at Goodfellow Air Force Base at 10 hundred hours. The Military Planes are capable of flying up in the stratosphere well over 1500 miles per hour; you get from point A to point B in no time. Once we got there we set up shack in the barracks, I always take bottom bunk. We have little time to get settled in then we have our briefing from Command Sergeant Major Anthony Thomas at 11 hundred hours.

"Morning men."

From whole company; "Morning"

"Our objective will be to neutralize the aliens with ground force. We will take Humvee's and Stryker's into Katy then Snipers will be spread out. As we move into Houston snipers will lead the way taking out enemy targets, and communicating with the rest of you when and how far to move. Once we reach this point putting you two kilometers away from Lucas Oil Tower, then you will settle a perimeter around the tower and keep your fucking heads on a swivel for space craft's they are flying by destroying the tower piece by piece with lasers from hidden chambers. They will practically vaporize your ass. They do lose power the further they travel, wear your flak jackets cause hit from long distance it has a good chance of saving your ass. Then you will attempt to shoot down their craft's hoping they still work somewhat with every craft taken down a team of decoders will try to figure out how to disarm the force fields. We have previously scanned the whole Houston area within a 30 mile radius for force fields there are zero." A few hoots and hollers are heard in the crowd. "The decoders will be traveling with us only in the Stryker's. There will be teams of three decoders. Once a craft is down the aliens don't like to see anyone going in them, they do destroy fallen crafts. A few men will need to stay by them and protect the decoders. We will leave at 18 hundred hours. It will be a little over 5 hours to Katy take your night vision, snipers use night vision scopes. These bastards aren't worried about camouflaging themselves they are ready for a fight let's bring it to them!" Lots of loud Hua and cheers rumble through the crowd. "Spend your time preparing for battle get some chow when you please. Be ready to move out at 18 hundred hours dismissed."

"HUA!" From the whole company.

Back in the barracks Mic cleans all his weapons one at a time he disassembles, cleans, oils, then puts back together. He inspects all his equipment and makes a mental list of all the backup ammo and other equipment he will need; then heads to the annex to pick it up. Once he has returned he does some floor exercises and gets some grub at 1330. He heads back to his bunk and does a quick video chat with his wife and kids. He lays down on his bunk takes out his bible and reads his favorite passages. Then he takes a quick 30 minute nap, when he wakes up he does more floor exercises then relaxes chatting with some of his platoon members. Once 1730 comes around he gets strapped up. After packing his rucksack with his essential shovel, rope, sleeping blanket, flash light, night vision goggles, a M.R.E, an extra bottle water, extra jackets for his M249 S.A.W, M16 and 9mm, then he equips his gun belt. On his left hip he straps his Berretta 9mm in front of that his wound pouch, that has gauze, bandage, sewing needle and thread and wound cleaner. On his right hip proper backup ammo, since he first will be leading the way as a sniper its backup clips for his M110 sniper rifle. Behind that his canteen. And strapped to his right leg his trusty knife. His S.A.W is slung around him for when they set up the perimeter. Once inside the Stryker he is assigned he sets his S.A.W to the side along with his rucksack and M110. He feels a greater sense of pride being assigned with a disarming team.

"I may just take a nap on the way out." Mic says to a scientist wearing his helmet in the armored vehicle.

"What if something happens to our Stryker?"

"There hasn't been alien air craft in this area the air force has checked."

"There could be some flying right now."

"If they fire on us it will barely pierce the armor."

"What if they hover right over us and fire?"

"That's not likely to happen we would hear them coming."

"Good point."

"Thanks you and the other decoders can take off your helmets, relax a while we got five hours before things get a little dangerous."

"Yea it's a little hard to relax knowing things will get dangerous."

"I agree but you have to do stuff to take your mind off it . . . do you have kids?"

"Yes six. Three boys and three girls."

"I have all three girls."

"Oh how lovely."

"Thanks. Congratulations on your six."

"Thanks. You too."

"So how long have you worked for NASA?"

"19 years."

"What did you study in college?"

"I went to Georgetown; I double majored in advanced communications and astronomy. Then to Harvard for my doctorate in astrophysics."

"So your pretty good at doing what you do and you know exactly what you're doing."

"Yea."

"I'm very good at doing what I do. I know exactly what I am doing, stay close to me everything will be fine. Not so close you're a distraction, but when we get out there do what you do best and I will do what I do best and we will kick ass.

"Sounds good!"

Mic ends up falling asleep but only for a half hour when he wakes up there is still three hours to go so he puts on his favorite music to pump him up. He starts with some heavy rock then some soul music to remind of all the nice things in his life and continues that mix up for an hour and a half, till he gets tired of listening to music. Then he strikes up conversation again with his new intellectual friend.

"You guys went through some military or officer training right?"

"Yea. We did eight weeks of officer training which to what I understand is just like military training."

"Yea it is exactly military training they made it so officers have to go through eight weeks of basic military training to be well rounded with various rifle and fire arms as well as hand to hand combat. Then to be a basic officer you go through officer school where you run drills and learn basic interrogation and investigation skills. Then if you stay in long enough and want more advance training they put you through what is equivalent to army infantry training.

"What are you, you're a special agent right?"

"Yep. I was in the Marines first then about a year and a half in I did recon and then sniper training. I was a sniper for three years then I continued advancing my training. Then my company commander told me about the National Security Agency looking for new recruits for policing units that would be more advanced and elite than any other such agency in the past. We replaced the C.I.A

"Oh yea the C.I.A hasn't been around for 31 years."

"We're more elite and stay involved in just America; we don't worry about overseas."

"Well luckily America hasn't been in a war in over 45 years."

"Now we find ourselves fighting new enemies, but the whole world is involved."

"They may have gills and tails and lasers but we will kick the dog crap out of them."

"Amen to that."

The scientist seems like he can rest at ease now. He feels even more confident in his own tasks. Mic goes back to listening to his soul and heavy metal to pump him up so more. Then gears up right before they get to their checkpoint. Mic puts on his rucksack before jumping out, he runs to position the men accompanied by the Stryker have to sit and wait till Mic gives the all clear. Mic runs up a couple hundred yards over the radio he reminds the other snipers to periodically check behind them and be alert of the advance stealth above them. As he advances he spots two on top of a hill, he dives for the ground. He doesn't know if they saw him, he quickly dials in his scope they are 750 yards away he takes aim and pulls the trigger, he busts him right in the head. The other alien tries to locate where the shot came from but wastes no time and flees. Mic fallows him with the scope and pulls the trigger; hits him right in the back. Mic likes the easier judgment call not having to determine if he's armed or not if he sees an alien he's killing it. He double times it in the same direction he goes only a hundred more yards before he spots another one. Once again he lies down, takes aim, the alien is 900 yards away, he pulls the trigger, another head shot. He radios to the Stryker and the rest of the platoon you're good for at least two clicks. Mic continues to double time it. He makes it a few more clicks before he decides to walk. The Stryker waits as he strolls closer to the city. He makes it a few more clicks without interference. Now since he knows he is within 4 miles of the city he takes a moment to collect himself.

"Ok" he thinks out loud. He takes out his map and flash light then on the radio says;

"We're three and a half miles from Houston. Snipers give your squad a minute to catch up." He hears over the radio from one the platoon members; "We will be where you're at in one and a half minutes."

"Good you're exactly where you need to be, take your time. Hernandez take your squad around the Toyota Tower come in from the East, Roth take your squad you guys come in from the South my squad will go in from the West, Anderson you guys from the North East and Jones you guys from the North West. We will wait get yourself ready for heavy gun fire and close combat. Let me know when everyone is in position and ready to go, we will all move in at the same time understood?"

"Roger." From every squad leader.

Mic disassembles his rifle and tucks it away in his rucksack and takes out his M249 S.A.W. He assembles his machine gun and locks a full magazine in. He puts a spare magazine in his ammo pouch on his belt. He also has two more that he put last in his rucksack so they're right on top. It is now habit for him to take a glance at his knife, one because he can see his reflection and two he gives the blade a feel to reassure it's very sharp. He puts it back and tightens the strap around his leg. He takes a big chug from his canteen and just as he puts it away he gets word from all squad leaders; ready to move out. Shortly after they get on the move they all can hear scattered gun fire as well as saucers circling around. As they get closer to the Toyota Tower sounds of chaos get louder and louder. They reach a mile and three quarters away from the tower and the gun fire starts. Mic, along with many other platoon members start taking out aliens from three to four hundred yards away. They move in closer, an alien craft flies past Mic's squad, a couple of soldiers try shooting it down but come up empty handed. Then another coming from the opposite direction fires lasers as it circles by; it doesn't hit anyone. The platoon scatters. "Don't get too far away keep a lookout for one and other." Mic shouts over the radio. Off to the west a saucer hums by Hernandez's squad they fire at hitting it multiple times but it seems to not phase the alien craft. Then from the North East Anderson's squad takes out a big chunk of alien air craft with a rocket launcher. It quickly crashes to the ground, the decoders deploy and receiving cover fire from the squad they head to the space ship. The injured aliens inside stagger out and are quickly wasted by the soldiers. However as the decoders approach; another space ship flying by unloads a bulk of lasers at it destroying the craft completely. The teams march on they are now a mile away from the tower. They can see that a quarter of the Toyota Tower is destroyed, along with many puncture wounds in her. By now the area is swarmed with ground force aliens and flying alien craft. They continue trying to take out as many aliens with as little collateral damage, all the while dodging alien space ship fire. The decoders from Anderson's squad see broken up alien craft that some civilians took down earlier they run to it. Aware of what could happen they cautiously approach the ship. Two of the six decoders go inside the aliens fly by very close blasting the ship to pieces with their lasers. Mic and his crew witness the atrocity. Mic can't help but think to himself; "that craft was right above them what a stupid time to go in the fallen space craft." He is angered now. Even though he doesn't want his emotions to get the best of him, it fuels him. Out the corner of his eye he sees a big nasty looking alien bearing down on some locals so he takes aim holds down the trigger and unloads six shots to its face and head. He then takes cover in an old abounded alley that is just a block shy of the tower. He listens closely waiting for a craft to fly threw the opening between the two buildings surrounding him; he knows his window of opportunity is small. He can hear one coming over the building he has his back to. He can hear it slowed down for the civilians on top; the second it comes to view he unloads nailing it at least 20 times as it flies by. He knows they have a hard time firing at anything directly below them so he runs around the side of the building he sees it crash land in the 10th floor of the Toyota Tower. He radios to his team of decoders. "We will go in through the south entrance up the stairs then trout down to the north side where it is wrecked." He waits for them at the entrance. The entrance is big enough to handle hundreds of people going in or out at one time the entrance alone takes up almost half a block. They all hurry in unscathed. Mic leads them to the stairs they hurry up at first then slow down remembering it's on the 10th floor. Keeping strategic formation as they make their way up the staircase Mic thinks they have done good remembering instructions on safe distances but wishes they would be quieter; just then the exit door busts open the decoder Brad comes face to face with an alien he freezes up; that's all he has time to do. The alien swipes Brad's head off with his long razor sharp claws. Mitch who is right behind him takes aim against the hand rail, he holds his trigger down for a second hitting the alien multiple times in the shoulder but the alien keeps coming after him, Mitch's eyes get real big he takes a deep breath in and before he can let it out squeezes the trigger again this time not letting go till the alien is sitting in a pool of purple blood. They keep heading on reaching the 10th floor. They take a look down the hall it appears to be empty Mic takes the lead once again. They reach the crash site; it went through the ceiling of one apartment, knocked down the hallway wall and landed on the kitchen floor across the way. As it ripped thru the ceiling it must have knocked the upstairs fridge out of place because as it was lying there on the floor with the fridge on top. It lay there blocking the aliens escape hatch and a smashed in sink blocked the other door. They must push the fridge off to get in. Decoder Aaron agrees to handle that business. Aaron climbs on top, squats down he sets his rifle down beside him and not knowing if an alien is waiting for it to be moved so it can get out; he shoves the fridge with all his might and bravery. The fridge crashes onto the counter top below him. Nothing happens, he cautiously approaches the door. Aaron slowly turns the hatch then pulls it open the door is heavy so he tries to gently let it rest. He takes a look inside, it is very dark, he leans a little closer, then all of a sudden an alien jumps up "AAAWWWWW" Aaron screams as leaps back, he reaches for his rifle. The alien lunges forward biting him and latching on to his face. Aaron lets out a blood curdling scream. The alien brings his tail over top and thrusts it midway into the side of Aaron's neck the scream turns to a quiet gurgle. Mic acts quickly and fires rounds into the side of the aliens head and neck killing it instantly. The alien lies lifeless on top of Aaron. The team moves the corps, they need to stay on track no time to mourn, not right now anyway. This time Mic takes a peak down into the alien air craft with pistol drawn he gets out his flash light; he can see two bodies motionless in chairs. He does not want to take a chance; he shoots booth of them in the head then gives the O.K for two decoders to move in. Each rung inside the space craft is very far apart suitable for the aliens.

They take a look around with the aliens dead they rest easy. It takes booth of them using all their strength to move the one that appears to be in the captain's chair; he had the most controls in front of him. Just as they go to work on figuring out the controls, a laser blast from close up destroys more of the condo. Mic yells "Get out of there!" They scurry out as fast as they can, jumping to the ground and take cover. Mic heads to the opening in the wall and hides behind some rubble he peeks out and as soon as he sees the other craft flying by; he blasts it out of the sky with his grenade launcher attachment sending it straight to the ground, it crumbles and smashes to pieces. The decoders hop back in the craft for a second try. They are able to work for a couple minutes before they are interrupted by another alien attack. This time they are ruthless with their lasers. They hit the fallen craft directly in its back the blast knocks both men head first into the dash board, the impact kills Dan. Adam, bleeding from the mouth and head staggers out the escape hatch. With his hands holding himself up he tries to lift legs out in front of him so he can slide down off the space craft feet first, but wasting that much time he gets blasted in the back with a laser powerful enough to vaporize his upper half sending his legs freefalling back down the hatch. Mic and the rest of the team can hear them hit the ground. The team must deal with this alien craft flying much faster and closer than the one previous. The team takes firing positions, the remaining two decoders huddle behind a wall. They're both so scared deep down they are hoping the team is not successful in protecting the fallen craft. They are in luck the speedy air craft demolishes it with a few laser blasts as it dashes by. Mic takes a peak out doesn't see anything close by. "Time to move out." He directs his team to the stairs they came up, they move out where they came in, the remainder of the team lines up against the tower. They survey the open field; there are lots of dead bodies. They notice it's quite, it seems as the fighting has seized. Then the unmistakable noise of more alien air craft's approach.

There is three circling high above the tower. At that distance they don't pose a great threat; Mic decides not to take aim and instructs his team not to either. Mic calls over the radio;

"Whats your 20?"

"My squad is lined up on the East side of the tower." States Hernandez

"We are a quarter mile from the south side, the south entrance, and approaching." Says Anderson.

"I see you Von Haus."

"That's you Roth."

No answer from Jones.

"Jones . . . Jones." Still no answer from Jones. "Roth move west take Jones' position Anderson you and Roth move in with caution."

"Roger."

Then command radios in. "22 command to Von Haus."

"Go ahead 22 command."

"Jones is dead along with half the squad, however all six decoders remain. We have instructed the remainders to continue moving in and to meet you."

"Roger, thank you 22 command. Head count, Hernandez."

"All still standing."

"Roth . . ."

"Minus two and minus one decoder."

"Anderson . . ."

"Minus three and minus one decoder."

"Roger."

"22 command to Von Haus."

"Go ahead."

"We are scattering Jones' team and sending the decoders to you."

"Roger . . . how far out?"

"Three quarter mile."

"Roger."

The alien air craft's continue flying overhead. They rotate around and around the tower. Starting at the top and working their way down. They target civilians fighting from their windows. Mic and Hernandez's team dodge fallen debris. The tower is slowly collapsing around them. Mic and his team formulate a plan.

"We are going to the Western corner we will stay on the north side, then one at a time, me first with you four decoders, I'm running out 30 yards North and 30 yards East, you four decoders stay close to the tower. Jake, you stay here with them. Rico you will run out to me then I will go 30 and 30 more, Williams then you run out to me and so on. Putting me 300 yards from the tower; creating a half circle around this side. I will pick a space ship closest to us the idea is to have it land in the middle, or whichever group of decoders it lands closest to needs to run out and save the day OORAW."

"YEA!" The whole team shouts.

"Once I start firing everyone decoders too, then it will start to target us so once that happens run your ass off to some cover OORAW."

A mixture of "Yea" and "OORAW" from whole team. They run out, take their positions, Mic doesn't waste any time the first one to circle to the North side he opens fire. The whole team fallows Mic and the rest of the team are relentlessly accurate. Before the space ship can even turn its attention to them it comes crashing down to the ground. It lands close to Mic and his decoders they run out to it. Mitch who killed an alien earlier is confident and is eager to be the first to get to the fallen space ship. Mic climbs a top the space ship the rest of the team provides cover fire at the other space ships that periodically turn their attention to soldiers. Hernandez's team on the East side starts experiencing casualties three members are hit with lasers. A fourth member is hit from a distance in his flak jacket it burns him badly but he is not taken out of the fight he lies on the ground in agonizing pain but as the pain subsides he jumps back up and open fires on the saucer that hit him. He hits it with numerous rounds from his M16 then hits it with a blast from his grenade launcher attachment.

The dude feels like Rambo. It comes spiraling down, he and a few others dive out of the way as it crashes into the tower behind them. Just inside the tower were three civilians who could not move in time. Their bodies lie motionless under the ruble. One was unfortunate to have the air craft land on her. They feel reluctant getting it down. One squad member opens the hatch and drops a smoke grenade in. They're not even sure if the smoke will have effect, it doesn't matter the three aliens inside are all dead. Meanwhile Mic takes cautionary fire then signals for two decoders to head in. Mic decides to stay on top the space ship and provide cover fire from there. He notices to the West an air craft go after Roth's team. They do what they can to return fire but Mic and his team just witness half of Roth's team get wasted in a matter of just a few seconds. The space ship launches higher circling back around the top of the tower again. Then from way high up come in two more air crafts to replace the two that are down. While they begin they're assault, Steve; the decoder Mic was talking to on the way out brings an issue to attention.

"There's no force fields around to shut down."

"Maybe there's one code to get rid of all the force fields." Replies Mic. "Besides you need to find out as much as you can about the space ships, now hurry up!"

The space ship that went after Roth's team came back to the tower. More and more of the tower is destroyed every minute. Mic thinks it will topple any moment but what he doesn't realize is all the towers were designed to crumble from the outside in, in the event of an attack. The outside is very solid but not as reinforced as the core. However once the core is left standing then it could topple from the ground up. After buying the decoders five minutes to find out what they can, he orders the platoon to reassemble 1000 yards away from the tower. With the space ships moving as fast as they are from that distance the platoon is not doing much damage. Mic focuses in on one space ship takes a deep breath and unloads; he empties the remainder of his clip on the space ship. The pelts just anger the alien air craft. It comes directly at Mic, not towards the squad but directly at him.

"Everyone armed with a rocket launcher prepare to fire." Mic says over the radio. "Hold off till its close enough for a good shot."

Without a signal all four are launched at the same time. The platoon watches; three of four hit the space ship. The fourth lands a couple hundred yards behind Anderson's squad. The fiery pieces fall out of the sky like drifting pieces of amber. The platoon is elated.

"One down two to go, let's move in 100 yards rocket launchers stay back and reload."

The platoon blasts a second one down with machine gun fire but before it fell its partner took out a chunk of the platoon. It went after Anderson's squad after wiping out eight men. Then it turned its attention to Hernandez's platoon it came right for them killing three. A couple of rockets launched at it but both missed. The space ship changed course and headed back to the tower. It delivered a devastating punishment finishing off the top deck. As it continued to circle the tower like a shark circling prey Mic ordered everyone to move in a little closer; they were in much better range now. The air craft sustained a lot of damage but was still on the rampage. Finally another synchronized rocket assault brought the master of disaster down. Mic chills out under some shade provided by some ruble. Mic takes a look around and surveys the carnage. He quickly gazes at his weapons for inspection, then chugs most of his canteen. Roughly 50 yards behind him in the crumbled tower officers Chet and Stevens chew the fat.

"This is crazy." Says officer Chet.

"Boy you can say that again." Replies officer Stevens. Just then a local comes down from the stair case.

"Holly crap." Says Chet.

"What?"

"That scared me. I forgot there's still people in here. And it makes it even more difficult to believe with all the dead bodies around."

"How long do you think this war will go on for; years."

"I would say at least a year or more, like two or three but who knows."

"What are they doing here, why are they starting all this?"

"The latest speculation is their planet is over populated and they're using force to colonize our planet and impose their lifestyle on us."

"It seems so simple but so far away; it's hard to wrap your mind around."

"I agree the enemy is so foreign but the idea isn't."

Then a large group of people; some wounded; some carrying wounded, come out. They seek aid, fresh air, and comfort. They mosey on by Chet and Stevens. As though they're not sure what to do with themselves they wonder into the open. They are accompanied by some the soldiers and decoders. They give them drinks of water and offer any kind of helping hand or comfort. Chet and Stevens stand at the entrance of a hole to the outside. They look around to see what they can do. Then an alien leaps out from a hole in the wall just behind them. It charges right at them catching them off guard it lashes its tail at Chet. He ducks under it just in the nick of time but he is unable to avoid the alien plowing into him with its shoulder. The momentum makes the alien fall forward but he braces himself and stays on his feet. Stevens runs over for where he sat his rifle the alien fallows closely behind. He attempts to out maneuver the alien and changes direction right before he gets to the rifle. It works the alien runs right past. With adrenaline pumping he runs faster than ever threw a door and into the hallway. He can hear the alien gaining on him he desperately yells for help, but receives no response. He yells again; louder. The alien reaches out with his hand trying to grab him. The alien just barely touches him on the shoulder. Stevens is very frantic now. "HELP ME!" He cries out. Then out the corner of his eye, he notices a blasted hole in the middle of the wall. Without thinking or hesitation he dives through head first. He lands on his shoulder cutting it badly on the broken mirror scattered on the floor. He rolls onto his back in time to see the alien peeking through the hole. The alien kicks and jabs making at the hole making it big enough for him to duck threw. Stevens is frightened he thinks this is the end for him. "HELP!" The alien stands over him. Stevens lies their defeated, the alien leans in closer, it raises its hand up high, but before it can slash down Stevens pulls out his knife to block it. The blade meets the alien's fingers. With severed fingers it is very pissed off. Stevens leaps to his feet. Stevens lunges at the alien with the knife. The alien jumps back and Stevens' slips and starts to fall, but the alien catches him by the throat. It closes his fingers around his neck and squeezes. The pressure breaks Stevens' windpipe. He gasps for air then goes limp in the alien's hand. The alien releases him and he drops to the ground. Chet had tried to catch up to them however when he gets their; he sees the alien standing over Stevens. Chet pulls out his side arm and with a whole gang of soldiers coming up behind him he unloads on the alien; five shots to the body. The alien falls back. Chet stands over the alien and pulls the trigger; he shoots it in the head. One would have been enough but Chet is not satisfied. He screams "AAAAHHHHHH!" as he empties the rest of the clip on him.

"Let's go." Another soldier says to Chet. "They just radioed; a security unit will be here in three hours, we are going to hit the road when they get here."

"Where are we going?"

"I think north, but don't worry about that now, let's rest and get some chow."

Once they get back outside a supplies humvee pulls up and passes out M.R.E's. Chow time can be very therapeutic; it can strike up some interesting conversations. After chow time and clean up some soldiers lay in the dirt with their faces covered by their hats. Others buddy up in the shade discussing sporting topics and how they can't wait for the security unit to get there. A few soldiers gather to toss a football around and bull about their favorite kills. Then one soldier tosses the football high up in the air and for the first time they notice six more alien air craft's closing in on them. They scatter for their rifles and other weapons. The aliens launch a heard of lasers at the soldiers. The soldiers return fire. Mic rallies his squad behind some fallen rubble a little ways away from the action. He notices one of the decoders has his rifle but no ammo.

"Where is your ammo?" Mic shouts.

"In my rucksack . . . at the bottom."

"Turn around." Instructs Mic. He pulls open his rucksack and starts pulling everything out; he doesn't find more ammo at the bottom. Mic hollers at a squad member; "Riggs, give me your grenade." Riggs tosses it to him. "Stay hidden this is your only hope." Hernandez and what is left of his team huddle against the tower spread out. A saucer flies by and opens fire, two of Hernandez's are hit and vaporized; a third is hit in the fore arm and losses it all the way to the shoulder. The rest of them take off along the tower, laser blasts fallow close behind. Roth and his men are scattered out in the open taking fire at a swooping alien air craft. The space ship picks them off one at a time. As the saucers fly by Anderson's team is scattered under cover at the far end of the tower trying to help take down the assassin, but they have their own to deal with. Having everyone on one side of the tower makes it easy for the aliens to take them out along with the tower. Mic knows this and orders his team to rush around to the other side.

"Stay low and move fast." Using debris to cover as they move into position they lose only one man. His team fires at two crafts that shift back and forth obliterating the south side of the tower. There is one space ship on booth the east and west side of the building and two more on north side. From Mic's team the gun less decoder decided to stay put. He first thought about throwing up the grenade as a diversion from Roth's team but quickly realized that would cost him the ultimate sacrifice. He knows he must wait for the right moment. Roth's team is now down to just him and two others. Anderson's team is getting hit pretty bad as well. His team is down to him and four others. Meanwhile Hernandez's team looks like they're on a hot plate trying to make it to the east side of the tower; which has sustained the least amount of damage. Finally on the east side there is not much to hide behind so they make their way to a corridor, and get inside. The remaining six from his team part to both sides of the hall and rotate turns shooting threw the open door. They shoot till they run out of ammo then to the back of the line to reload. None of the teams have had much luck with six very strategic flying space ships. Now as the tower continues to crumble they have to worry about it toppling over. The space ships have already blasted through layers and layers; it won't be long till the tower collapses from the ground up. The sol decoder is scared. He thinks if he could take off running towards his team one might chase after him and he could hurl the grenade at it. He decides to give it a try. He takes off as soon as he notices the space ship coming at him his adrenaline kicks in; lasers swarm around him, then he changes direction just barely dodging a laser. He sprints to a boulder to take cover; he dives but while still in the air; he gets hit in both legs just above the Achilles. He lies face down in agonizing pain. He turns over on his back just in time to see it hovering in front of him. He rips the pin out, waits for a second then tosses it at the space ship. Before it explodes the aliens douse him with lasers. The grenade explodes but not close enough to the space ship. Mic and his squad are having a blast dealing with alien air craft's. They have hit both several times but from far away, nothing penetrating deep enough to do major damage. Right around the corner Hernandez and his crew are still rotating pot shots but mostly watching the walls vanish around them. In the open Roth displaying great poise manages to land several hits on his target. Between himself and some guys from Anderson's squad they shoot down a space ship. There are two decoders left with Anderson six left with Hernandez and seven left with Mic. Roth radios to Mic to send decoders to him.

Hernandez says he can get him two. Roth tells him Anderson's two are already almost at the sight. The two from Anderson's crew hop in cautiously; all three aliens are dead inside. While they go to work Mic and his team gun down another one. A vicious exchange of lasers and gunfire brings down a third after it takes out everyone in Anderson's team leaving him by himself. Hernandez sends in two of his decoders to go to work and tells Anderson to come join him. Anderson doesn't want to leave though the little rock he has been behind has brought him good luck so far. Roth however has had enough of being out in the open and hurries to join Hernandez. On his way he gets a crystal clear shot of a space ship concentrating on Hernandez and his crew so he unloads sending the space ship crashing down. It did not fall far so just as Roth gets there two decoders proceed with caution. One looks down the hatch they appear to be dead. He jumps down. No movement. He turns around to see what he can figure out and an alien leaps out of his chair at him. Before the decoder can turn around the alien lashes at him with his tail; thrusting it threw his lower back and out his stomach. He lets out a piercing scream. His partner quickly reacts, shooting it in the head. He jumps down and rifles a couple rounds into the pair of cronies. His buddy is not dead but dying. He radios for medical assistance right away. The focus is now keeping his partner alive. He can see the large hole in his back all the way to the small opening in his front. The wounded decoder has passed out from pain. It is a little easier to treat the wound without loud chilling cries. He remembers to keep pressure on the wound. When he puts his hands over the wound he can feel them sink in. It freaks him out. He does his best to bandage the opening. He covers both the front and back then proceeds to wrap his whole waist with gauze and more bandages. He runs out of ideas. Shortly after he is done wrapping him he can see the blood seeping through. Then 22 command lets him know the security unit is a half hour out and will be there with medics and doctors. By the way the bandages are soaked he knows it's a loss. His spirit is raised but his soul sinks. For the first time he feels the heavy burden of a fallen friend. Outside the shooting and dodging continue. Mic launches a grenade with perfect timing and location, down goes number five. One more to blast out. Mic and his crew rifle off like target practice at the sol space ship in the sky. They send it crashing down to the ground shattered to pieces between them and Hernandez's crew. That's when the National Guard security unit comes pulling up. When it seems peaceful and at ease, then the decoder climbs out of the space ship with no choice but to leave his former friend. The troops quickly load up in the Humvee's and Stryker's. Since much less people are being transported the few Humvee's and Stryker's not being used stay back and are donated to the security unit. Steve the decoder Mic was talking to on the way out; happens to sit next to him again. Just after they get going they hear the tower crumble. They all look back and only see the east side of the tower left standing.

"Hey I didn't catch your name."

"Steve."

"Nice to meet you, Steve."

"Thanks you too. What's your name?"

"Mic."

"Do you know where we are going?"

"Yes, we are going north to Dallas. There is a tower there bigger than that one that just collapsed." Steve nods. He knows. He's from Dallas but does not bother to mention. "It hasn't been under attack yet but it could be when we get there." Steve is thinking it will be nice to show him something from his old neighborhood if he gets the chance. Mic goes on about what to expect.

"There are three force fields staggered between here and there. The space ships will be close by. They will sneak up; they will be utilizing their best stealth. We will be the largest group passing threw in a long time. This is where in a hurry or without warning things could go bad. They could be looking for us. If they spot us they will come up;" Mic does a diagram with his hands. "So quietly and unload on us, blasting us to pieces before we even see them flying off. Then again they may not check the highway they may be on the hunt for soldiers or people on foot in the fields and woods. If we can make it all the way without hassles it's just over three hours, actually at the rate these Stryker's go it will be more like four hours."

"Yea I can't wait." He decides to break the news to him. "I'm from Dallas. I know there have been a couple of space ships flying around. I wouldn't be surprised if they were under attack when we get there, and they probably won't let us know."

"No, they would let us know. It's being monitored right now, and no reports that an attack has been started."

"Yea, but the power has been down for almost the whole tower since yesterday so they may not know."

"Yea, it has been hostile but we will know when we get there, or before."

As they ride on, back at Mic's house things are peaceful. His girls attend to their crops in the green house and mom keeps the house clean and the food well cooked. Ray comes over from next door, to visit and see how things are. When he comes in just Debra is in the house; she just finishes in the bathroom and notices Ray standing in the kitchen.

"Hey Ray, you need anything?" Ray just shakes his head.

"You look nice in that sweater."

"Thanks. It's not that bad today."

"Yea, not very cold."

"What do you and Janice have planned for dinner?"

"Nothing particular. I like seeing you Deb."

"Thanks . . ."

"You're very pretty and you got some sass to you. As you know we have been cooped up . . . I got to tell you I'm jealous of you and Mic."

"Oh flattering, how so?"

"He gets to be with you every night." Ray looks around.

"I think you better leave Ray."

"You look so fun to be with."

"Ray, just stay away!"

Ray studies her body language for a second, then goes to make his move. He runs up to her and grabs her by her hips. She squirms; when he tightens his grip she head butts him in the nose. She runs to her freezer; remembering where she just left a hunk of frozen meat grabs it and whips it at his head just as he takes off in her direction. She hits him so hard it knocks him to the ground. She scrambles to the pick up the meat off the floor. She stands over him threatening to hit him again. He just lies there dazed and in pain, she hurries over to her drawer and pulls out a butcher knife she gets on her tippy toes to see him beneath the counter lying there defeated. She keeps a firm grasps on the knife. Without his pride and dignity he gets up and leaves with his head sunk low. As he is almost through the back door Debra yells;

"Yea keep walking! Get lost!"

She thinks he is going home to face whatever discipline Janice dishes out. Debra needs to do something to get what happened off her mind, so she heads to the sink, she starts to clean dishes that are already clean. She gets a towel to dry the ones she just rewet and looks out her window just in time to see ray make a B line to the force field. Her eyes get real big her mind races as she watches him run into the force field. Not sure if Janice saw what happened out her window she rushes over to the radio she gets ready to call her but hesitates to think about what to tell her. She wants to hysterically tell her everything but a small part of her thinks does his family need to know his motive, or can they think it was a freak occurrence, another alien casualty. Then she thinks did anyone from his family know he was coming over. If they knew he was over then she would have to tell them what their father and husband tried. Then a moment of clarity for Debra she knows not to hide the truth. But then they might blame her. For what; she thinks. It may not be best for their family but it's the right thing to do. As gently as she can she tells Janice her husband ran into the force field. She figures she will wait to tell the motive but if she questions why; she will be upfront with her then. Janice and Debra make arrangements for father McDaniel to come out and do the service. On the second day after Ray's death they are mid way thru the funeral precession at their house when Debra notices an alien in the back yard. Debra grabs the girls and runs for the safety of her house. Janice, her family and father McDaniel rush in behind them. Debra grabs weapons and passes them out they look out the window for it and see it coming right for them so they hurry to the hide out; all except Debra who is armed and ready to go. She wants to see if he tries to come in. She watches it out her kitchen window. The alien suddenly disappears; it uses its ability to turn its skin any color to camouflage its self with all the colors in the yard; it is virtually invisible. Debra tries tracking its movement, but it has disguised that as well. She just keeps her focus on the back door; the second it tries coming in she is going to unload. Her eyes are fixed on the door she has waited for five minutes now she doesn't want to move because she is worried that checking out a window give up her position and give it a chance to bust in while her back is turned. No she must maintain discipline. For five more minutes she stays crouched out of sight, with her eyes glued to the back door. BOOM, pieces of the front door hit the ground. From where she is at in the kitchen she leans over trying to look through the fresh hole in the front door. She sees nothing. BOOM! Another larger hole to look through, Debra stands fully erect, with her gun aimed out in front of her. She makes her way into the living room, she inches towards the door. BOOM, the door flings open. Nothing is there . . . then she hears footsteps racing at her; she fires her 8mm four times; the footsteps stop. She waits; within a second of hearing a loud thud the alien appears lying on the ground in a pool of blood. CRASH! She is startled and turns around; a really big alien is standing in the sliding back door frame with shattered glass all around it. The alien hisses at Debra. It wants to intimidate, but she charges at the alien and it runs at her, she meets it with a drop kick to the mid section knocking the alien flat on his butt. She scrambles to her feet as the alien hurries to his. He attempts to charge over her but is too tall she sees him coming and slides under on her knees tripping him up, he stumbles and crashes to the ground. He quickly springs back up. Debra takes aim and fires, she hits the alien in the chest, but it keeps coming after her unfazed. Before she can get off another round it reaches back and with one powerful swipe with its long arm it knocks her gun out of her hand breaking her middle finger in the process. She backs up it fallows she backs up more it fallows. She jabs at it but it does not flinch. Against the counter she is out of room and it is two feet away standing over her. It yells to intimidate, but Debra keeps her cool and does not move. Again the alien reaches way back and just as it sends it's arm forward she ducks making the alien hit nothing but air. She can see anger come over it's face. After she ducked she side stepped, she's going circle around this bastard. This time it swipes at her with a forehand but still hits nothing but air. This time it jabs at her with its claws but again hits nothing. She thinks for a second about the meat defense, but that plan is canceled when the alien slashes at her with his long spear tail that she barely evades by stepping back, she knows she doesn't want to be against the counter again so she needs to throw a strike of her own, she waits till he winds up for another one then charges in with her chin tucked down and smashes him in the chest with top of her head. Her blow barely knocks him back but creates enough room for her to dodge his long winded counter swipe. If she could duck under his next one then make a dash to the gun and ammo safe she can grab a knife and double her chances. Hear it comes she ducks under and brushes by the alien and yanks open the door which also provides a shield from another powerful blow. The aliens claws hit the steel safe door so hard the door slams back shut, but the blow came late she had already grabbed a buck knife from a holder in the door and squares off with the alien. The alien tries an upper cut, but Debra jumps back and uses the knife to block the blow. The alien gets cut real badly on the hand and fingers, it however still seems unfazed. It stalks her down the hall they pass by the bathroom, then Jasmine's room, then Stacy's room. She knows being in close corners is a bad idea so she must pick one of the two remaining rooms. She decides to dive into her room, Debra thinks its personal now fucker. Give me your best shot. Once the alien is in the door way before it can duck under and take a step inside; she lunges at it with the knife sticking it right below the chest. The alien lets out a yell this time in agonizing pain, and giving it no time to recover she stabs it again in almost the same spot. With her hands firmly around the knife she drives it into the wall behind it and yanks it out before the alien can react. She backs up and it staggers after her, the alien reaches back and before it can bring its arm forward she lunges forward thrusting the knife in its throat and back out dodging the swooping forehand. The alien falls face down. Debra bends down and lifts the alien's giant head to look in its eyes for a second; its eyes are lifeless. She gets this overwhelming sense of joy from defeating her enemy, but that is a buzz kill compared to the euphoric feeling she gets, knowing her kids are ok. She heads down and tells everyone it is safe to come out. Once everyone is gathered in the kitchen Debra suggests that her kids do some school lessons.

"Let's contact Mr. Johnston . . ." Debra says with a cool demeanor. "We should see if he is available to spend a few hours with you guys later this afternoon. You guys can go over some material over the next few days."

"That sounds good." Replies Stacy.

"I like Mr. Johnston." Says Jasmine.

"Yea, he's nice." Says Erica.

"You can do virtual lessons from 12 to 4 for the next two weeks . . . If he is available he hasn't seen you guys for over a month. All of you can get caught up on your studies."

Janice asks; "Do you need help moving those big bodies? Jeff and Darren can help you carry them down to the incinerator."

Debra doesn't answer at first then says; "No need." She just doesn't feel comfortable having them around. She doesn't mind letting them use her house as a safe nest, especially in the face of danger for the time being, Rays son is too much like him and she wants to limit people feeling like she owes them something in a time like this. Her girls are trying not to act impressed with mom's victory they know she wants to get back to business, so they are eager to help their momma. "If you don't mind I'm a little tired and have some injuries to attend to, we will be busy boarding our door. We will see you around, take care guys."

"Yea we will get out of your hair. Shall we leave?"

"We got our preparations to do. You girls ready?" Deb says to her daughters. "You guys have a good safe night." Deb walks them all out the broken door and says good bye to each one on their way out. After cleaning up and a couple of chores the family spends some good time together. Momma talks to Mr. Johnston and plans their educational agenda and goals for the next couple of weeks. Then spend the rest of the night watching their favorite TV shows together. They don't say much because everything that is on their mind they already know; and the only thing on their mind is how much they love each other. Over the next few days they stick to their strict agenda, and stay on high alert. Momma stays on gardening and cooking detail, and leaving the house is kept to a minimum. Mr. Johnston makes sure the virtual lessons are challenging for everyone. He tries to make the exams very challenging but the girls do a very good job keeping up with their studies. Ten days have gone by since the household invasion, and momma feels it's time to relieve some cooped up cognitions. And one of the best ways a women knows how without being able to leave the house is by a virtual shopping spree. Even with lots happening life must go on. Sexy lady number one and the girls buy it up; they buy everything from shoes, lingerie, clothes, accessories, jewelry, and entertainment. The little devils even indulge in forbidden desert; the finest of rare delectable's. Even when a girl is engulfed with new merchandise she can't help but wonder if her husband is ok.

Mic is ok, but he is moving closer to danger. They start formulating a strategy, and get word from command fighting has already started. When the team gets there theirs already the National Guard and Regular Army battling it out. They are going to try to take out two or more at a time to optimize time needed in the space ships. Mic along with a few others switch back to M110 rifles they are looking for precision targeting along with hundreds of troops utilizing M16 and S.A.W's. With much higher numbers their operation goes much smoother. With the snipers precision on the space ship engines and the infantry and ranger units punching holes left right and center they gun down three at once leaving two in the sky to wreak havoc on the troops on the ground and civilians in the American Tower in Texas. Mic keeps the space ships at bay as they turn their attention to the crashed space ships on the ground. The decoders are able to get plenty of work done. The two banged up space ships in the sky fly high to avoid being shot up. But after they do a lot of damage to the top of the tower they come down to take out some troops and attempt to level the tower. The troops are relentless in pursuit of gunning them down. After a brief onslaught the other two space crafts crash to the ground. The team does not celebrate just yet; though the decoders are plugging away they have not figured out a disarming code. With three force fields in the area they are very motivated. As expected more space ships come but after another brief assault five more lay conquered on the ground. They still aren't done five more with cloaking mechanism come in undetected. Not able to see their targets till a blast of lasers give off where they were; calls for aimless fire. They have to remain calm, keep cool and utilize all their senses to pinpoint their targets. After the space ships have subdued enough damage their cloaking mechanism gives out. For a little while the numbers were in the aliens favor. But now 15 space ships lie out of order. Their isn't even enough decoders from the original strike to occupy the immobile alien air crafts. Another intense, grueling battle leaves many to burry. After a brief rest and mourn they get good news that the secretary of defense ordered a deployment of Stratus Guard to join the battle. It will be advanced man air crafts V.S alien space ships. With good news comes bad news. An all out deployment means many, many more men and women are called to provide sacrifice from homes and families to war against aliens. The original assault crew gets word from command to hold steady till more supplies come and the aid of a base to provide rest for a day, before they head further north to the Great Plains to fight the masses on the ground. The decoders will be left behind; replaced with only a couple per platoon for when they encounter a couple space ships on patrol throughout the Great Plains. The hunt for space ships is over the war has just started.

Chapter 5

THE WAR

Shortly after the dust settles a unit of reservist shows up. They have aid and supplies equipped with the set up of dormitory trailers, mess hall tents, and command posts. After chow and R and R, the original crew of alien annihilators is briefed on what time they move out tomorrow. They are re-grouped with new additions to the team and one platoon of four moves out in the afternoon. That platoon spreads out east to get an early scope of the battle field. They will go ten miles east and five miles north then set up camp, then get a late start so the other three will catch up. Each platoon has two decoders and 30 men. Mic is the leader of 1st platoon. For most of the platoon it is easy to get a good night sleep because they are so exhausted. But others struggle because of reflection on everything that has happened so far and what they must set out to do tomorrow. In the morning Mic spends some time re dialing his scope and setting his sights. Before they leave all the soldiers get fully equipped.

Like a scatter plot all across the globe the Stratus Guard takes flight. I don't think the aliens knew we had lasers. Most civilians did not know we had lasers. Our militarized air mobiles are similar to their space ships. Ours are not round and are smaller. The militarized stratus mobiles run on jet fuel. The laser chambers are at the front, two on both sides. The lasers are mounted in the chambers and can rotate a 360 degree radius. They stretch out long enough to create a six foot diameter rotation. They are capable of five electromagnetic radiation emissions every second. Or laser blasts for short. These are what go against the more powerful, faster space ships. One advantage of our stratus ships is their mobility. Ours are quicker; they bank faster and on a dime. The alien space ship lasers aren't capable of rotating; so the space ship has to be pointed at its target. We call our crafts Stratus Ships because they are capable of operation in mesosphere but not across galaxies like our enemies. Our enemies shoot larger more powerful lasers but that's because they are limited to one blast per second then takes one full second to recharge. The space ships have four lasers each and can fire one right after the other or all four at once. After our five blasts per second it only takes half a second to recharge the electromagnetic radiation. So it's a large semiautomatic operant against a smaller rapid fire operant. Each Stratus ship is individually manned and every ones goal is simple. The goal or mission is to get way up in the stratosphere and go one on one; sending as many space ships crashing to the ground as possible. Everyone is sent out to do their best including

Jose Rejos who has been with the stratus guard since it got started 12 years ago.

Jose with all other deployments know that hovering in the mesosphere is a large mother ship housing all space ships. She has over 200,000 ready to go. And Jose wants to be the man to blast that bitch out of the sky. Her position is over the Atlantic. She sends her ships out east and west. Targeting the large cities first then the rural areas. It will not be Jose or any other individual taking out big momma. She is solid. She stretches over four football fields in length and is four stories high. Not only is she capable of releasing her minions but she can emit a laser blast powerful enough to boil the Atlantic Ocean or wipe a major city off the globe, whatever way she see fit. If threatened by missiles that may be exactly what she unleashes. Jose does not want to sit back and wait for the first wave to be wiped out; he is going after everyone, for all the marbles. Luckily everyone feels the same way; a hundred thousand air men are determined to do their part in saving the end of our civilization.

Before his first flight Jose along with many, many others kiss his wife, and works his way from youngest to oldest saying good bye. He promises a safe return home. He encounters his first two early in the clouds; they appear out of nowhere in front of him. "Whoa!" He banks hard left avoiding a collision with one. He circles around and fires at their backside before they can do an about face. He thinks this may be easy. It's not long before he is met by two more. They fly at him like it's a game of chicken. Booth the space ships fire at him first. They miss by a long shot. He blast's four at the one on his left then three to the one on his right. He then swoops to his left and splits between the two and quickly turns around. Now behind both of them the one on his right tries to turn around but can't and keeps flying straight. He quickly fires at the one on his left just before it can get turned all the way around and finishes it off. Jose chases after the other one that can only bank right. Once he is 200 yards away he fires three more lasers. He nails it directly in the back and banks hard right. He is able to see it heading straight for the ground. He however does not look long enough to see it roll over and fire a couple shots at him as it continues its collision course with earth. Jose almost flies into the path of one of the lasers blasts as he completes his whip around. "Whoa!" Is his favorite term to use. Time to continue his climb in altitude and seek out a few more. After he climbs a few more miles he travels east on the lookout for another victim. He quickly comes up behind one hovering. He has to slow way down to avoid hitting it. He blasts it from behind then flies straight up. He sees it falling so he levels out and seeks out another. He flies east for 50 miles before he meets two more who see him coming. As he gets closer he holds steady waiting to dodge a stream of lasers. The space ship out in front decides to fire first. It fires one after the other in sequence. Jose banks left then back right; curving around the lasers. He blasts all four of his own at once. It is a direct hit but from a distance so great it merely scorches the surface. He quickly shifts right and sends a rapid fire;

five lasers from all four at his next opponent. The space ship cruses to his right attempting to dodge the blast but can't get out of the way of all of them. Jose has to bank right. They chase after him. They could step on it and blast their space ship right threw him but he could dodge them and they would over shoot him, turning the tables sort of speak. So instead they slowly gain on him. He tries flying straight up but they match his maneuver and continue gaining on him. He levels out and quickly banks right trying to shake them. The space ship in the lead has to loop around but the space ship trailing stays on his path. Jose suddenly banks left and takes a nose dive. Like an inner tube behind a boat the space ship stays behind him. Jose is able to gain some distance. As he continues downward; the mass of the space ship alone helps it gain it back. Like a great white gaining on a seal it's ready to make its killer move. Just as it opens fire; Jose swerves right and barely dodges what would have been a fatal shot. Firing before it can react, cost the aliens, Jose knows this he continues whooping around hoping to put himself behind the aliens. He almost has them in sight but has to bail because the other space ship is about to intercept and cut him off. Jose has no choice but to nose dive and let him fallow. This time before too long he pulls up at full throttle. That is something the space ship cannot match. He gets way out ahead and now sharply banks right bringing him head to head with the trailing space ship. He quickly fires first. His flurry of lasers comes too quickly and nails the space ship right on the nose. It smolders and the ship goes down in pieces. The other space ship continues the chase. Just as it starts to gain on him again he shifts left, then back right, then right some more. Like a wide receiver against a corner back he is trying to make the space ship guess which way he is going to go. He nudges right then banks hard left. Once he straightens out the space ship is a great distance behind him. He knows another move like that and he can loop around putting himself in position to catch the space ship. He waits a moment and lets the space ship gain on him a little. Then he puts it full throttle and quickly banks left, looping around as fast as he can he finds himself playing fallow the leader. He doesn't want to tail to close because the space ship has not gone full speed yet and could exit the chase on a straight away. Knowing it may do that at any second; he carefully takes aim and sends a rapid fire with his inner two lasers. His fire nails it in the back side and clips the edge. Pieces of the ship break off but it is still flying. The space ship now has limited mobility and is losing speed. Jose advances right up to the space ship and repeats fire sequence. This time the lasers leave hardly any remains. Now he is on a war path to find more, but runs into a brick wall when he realizes he needs more fuel. He takes it down and calls it a day. He and his family live on base so goes home and makes a plan for tomorrow. The new Stratus Guard base that he has lived at for the past 12 years called Apollo Shield is not far from St. Louis, where he grew up. He plans to survey the Anheuser Busch Tower and pursue all in the playing field.

When he comes up on the tower there are two saucers flying ramped, interchanging one and other staying on one side of the tower blasting people in their apartments. From what he can see the saucers took target practice on people fleeing through the exits. Thousands of people scrambling to their air mobiles with their boyfriends, husbands, wives, and kids trying to escape but getting shot down. At least Jose is not alone. Shortly after he arrives other airmen in the area join him. Jose flips on his IRMP3 and plays his favorite ancient rock song "No More Mr. Nice Guy" by Alice Cooper; he is amped up and ready to go to work. He radios to his fellow airmen which one he is going after and commands flying positions so three of them can keep guard from above. He and another go head to head against the space ships. Jose circles around the building he is trying to time coming around the other side and pop out in the space ships face. When he pops out the space ship is right there as he planned. He pelts it with lasers, destroying the front end and wiping them out. His new aquatints does his part by flying way up high and getting over top the space ship and blasting it from above. The newly formed team flies in formation with three out in front and Jose and his partner staggered behind them. They climb in altitude and after a little while come across eight scattered over a mile stretch of air. The team takes first blast. After the shooting begins the five of them are surrounded in a three quarter circle of enemy air craft. Porter an airman for seven years does an about face and immediately goes after the one diagonal from him. As he takes off in a B line towards his target, the one to his left fires late and misses. Porter punches it towards his target. His target fires at him from long range. Porter shoots up and doges the laser. Then from a slightly downward angle he fires; smashing it in the nose. He then banks hard left to go after the jerk that fired at him. That jerk already started his charge after he missed and is hot on his tail. Porter always knows to check behind him and sees him coming up, so he goes full speed and climbs at a 90 degree angle. Since he can accelerate much faster than the space ship; this puts some distance between them and at the peak of that distance he pulls another about face and delivers a rapid fire that busts the space ship up. Jose takes out a target and two of them went on a chase. Their fifth member; named Jetson flies hard at two closing in on him. He approaches . . . he flies up dodging lasers; he flies down dodging more; they're getting closer, he shifts left, then right. They get closer still, then BOOM, BOOM, BOOM, BOOM, BOOM both explode simultaneously as Jetson splits through the fireballs and ruble. Jose and Porter get two to chase after them they cross route one and other on their escape. Then eventually separate and the space ship chooses to fallow Jose. But Porter pulls a you turn and is tailing the aliens. He communicates with Jose over the radio. "Bank right, NOW!" Porter firmly holds down his firing buttons sending a rapid fire from all four lasers. The aliens are completely vaporized. The three airmen hover around hoping for good news from the two that scattered on a chase. After a minute goes by

Jose is just about to order flying formation north when he hears on the radio from Franklin; "I'm coming back to meet ya."

"Hey Alright!" Jose calls out on the radio. Shortly fallowed by;

"Me too!" From Bennett. Now they can fly north. With all airmen back aligned they increase altitude to 90,000 feet. After journeying north for a while with no encounters they are coming up on the Metro Tower and have two options. They could decrease altitude and greatly lower risk being out numbered or stay where they are at and face ten to twenty. They agree to stay where they are at.

"I see a group, pacing above us." Jetson says on the radio.

"I see em; they are monitoring the Metro Tower." Says Bennett. "They will see us shortly." Right after he says that the space ships start their path right at them.

"Let's give them a taste." Says Jetson.

"WHOA!" Jose anxiously shouts. "There's ten of them that's two to one fellas two to one."

The team spreads out. All down the line they know which two they are taking on. Jose gets shot at first. He dodges the shots and quickly returns fire; firing one from each laser. He misses the space ship dodges his shot. Then all out shooting from both sides. As Jose gets closer he has to twist and turn his Stratus Ship. One space ship retreats flying in reverse to escape. Jose goes after that one. It slowly turns around to get on the run faster. But that cost it; Jose catches up and shoots it from behind and it falls to the ground. Once it reaches a certain point in the atmosphere it bursts into flames the rest of the way down. Jose then circles to the right as he completes his loop around a space ship is ready for him and fires lasers in his direction. He quickly and abruptly slows his speed and the lasers flash past him. He banks hard right, then hard left and opens fire with all four lasers nailing the space ship in its side. Two down he has done his part but time to check on his compadres.

Porter has already taken one out himself. He is currently chasing around another. Jetson pulling off some fancy flying got two to crash into each other. Bennett is caught between two. Jose spots him and comes to his aid. Bennett is dodging heavy bombardment. But then Bennett hears a loud BLAST. Jose picked off the space ship tailing him. Now he has to cap off the one he is chasing. Jetson joins the fight and now it is two to one against the aliens. Jetson forces the aliens towards Bennett. With nowhere to go they're an easy mark for Bennett. Porter fires at his target on the run. He clips the side of the space ship. It banks right as hard as it can. Porter fallows, it swerves to try to shake him. He keeps fallowing. A loud thunder as the space ship tries to propel itself out of there but Porter already pulled the trigger and the lasers blast it before it can shoot out of there. When the space ship falls it crashes threw the metro rails connecting Minneapolis to Chicago. Luckily the train on the tracks got word and was able to stop a hundred yards short of the wrecked tracks and reverses back to Chicago. Meanwhile Franklin is in the fight of his life. When some fellow aliens took off or chased an airman this space ship hovered till Franklin was tailing a space ship and tailed him. And after he shot it down, these aliens shot at him and clipped one of his engines. He decreased altitude and has been exchanging fire. Franklin and the aliens loop past each other they fire at the same time both get hit. Franklin's tail gets shot off. It puts him in a down ward spiral. The aliens floor it and get beside him and blast his space ship to pieces right before he goes for the eject lever. The remaining team members huddle together in the sky and decide to take it down. They land in an open field east of Minneapolis. Their plan for tomorrow is to head east to Milwaukee. With one less member of their crew they hope they can acquire another along the way. They will have to wait and see what tomorrow brings.

In the morning Mic and his platoon continue their campaign through the Great Plains. The morning dew makes the soldiers tip of their boots wet. They have made it to the northern part of Arkansas. The air is brisk. Fog comes from their mouths with every breath. The squads keep a steadfast pace as they strut through the grass land. The four platoons have maintained they're spread miles apart from east to west. They have only encountered minimal opposition. They sense they are due for a big battle. Each platoon fallows behind two surveillance droids. They record what is in front of them and relay the image to a hand held monitor carried by a surveillance specialist each platoon acquired a couple days ago. The droids are capable of detecting not only force fields but carbon, hydrogen, oxygen and nitrogen in a condensed form. That gives them early detection of rival forces in the area. As they make their way through the northern part of Arkansas they come up on a very dense forest area. It's known as Devils Den State Park. First platoon being the middle platoon and going through the densest part they proceed with caution. Third platoon being furthest east trudges on along the Arkansas and Oklahoma border. The name of that section of wilderness alone creates an eerie feeling. One of the droids they are fallowing gets stuck on a branch on the ground. The operator goes to extend the front leg so it can reach the first hinge and bend back and rest on the branch then slide forward till the wheel is released off the branch. Before the operator can start that process for its hind legs the monitor flashes a warning. Before he needs to check the warning he can see on the monitor three aliens looking right at the droid. He scans left to right to check how many there are. There are 15 or so scattered out, ready to fight. The operator signals to Mic what he sees. Mic signals to his platoon to halt, then to take specific positions. Mic switches to his M110. The droid relays exactly where all of the aliens are. Mic signals to the other two snipers in the platoon to take positions. Mic heads off to find a ridge to perch up on and scope out the situation for his self. He gets to his point and radios to the snipers to fire when they have a shot.

Judas is a great sniper, one of the best with a fifty caliber. He sits on top of his ridge. He can see a group of four putting on a fierce display of overwhelming strength and power. They hiss and announce in English, this is their territory. Before he can pull the trigger they get on the run and go to camouflage mode. Judas tries tracking them by watching the brush move. He can't take a shot because he is not sure if he will hit a darting target or the wind. He is agitated, he had one in sight but he hesitated because he wanted a head shot. His own cognizance has cost him.

Samuel another great sniper is ready for his shot. He has only one 600 yards from his fifty caliber. He takes aim for the middle of his chest. He takes a deep breath and pulls the trigger. From that range the fifty cal puts a hole in the beast the size of a basketball. But that's the only one to go down. The rest also went into camouflage mode. The platoon holds ground and at that very moment Mic receives word over the radio from second platoon's leader who is east of first platoon that they stumbled across fifty or more aliens. It is possible the aliens they sighted have covered enough ground already to rally with the others so Mic commands his platoon to track east to support the second platoon. They double time to join the fight. Mic finds a hill for him and the other snipers to gather on. They watch the action unfold. Troops set up to take fire at the aliens. In a staggered line the gun fire kills many aliens but many more once the shooting started commenced their camouflage skin. Mic, Judas, Samuel, and Donmir each take out one, then struggle to target anymore. They instinctively run down hill. Mic tucks his rifles away and pulls out his knife. As he is running he is met with a blunt force, he knows it is an alien but he cannot see it. Lying on his back he looks around. With his knife he hacks at nothing. Then he is picked up and smashed into a tree trunk then tossed on the ground. From the way he was thrown he has an idea of where the alien is at. He is looking right at it but he does not know it. He hears a twig break beneath the alien's feet. He now knows exactly where it's at. He hops to his feet, the alien knows he is spotted and reveals his self. They square off circling around each other. Mic makes the first move. He jumps and thrust his knife at the alien but lacks the proper reach. The alien charges Mic and wraps its hands around Mic's head and squeezes. Mic slashes it in the fore arm. It releases. The alien takes a swing at Mic, claws out. Mic blocks it with his knife. He takes another swing; Mic ducks it and sticks the alien in the leg. The alien takes another charge and with a closed fist and uppercuts Mic knocking him on his back. Mic is dazed and disoriented. The alien picks him up again, holding him above his head he smashes Mic into another tree trunk. Mic feels his ribs break. He gathers his composer and thrusts his knife into the same forearm he slashed. He thrusts it again, this time into the bicep. He leaves the knife in there and the alien drops Mic. Despite the pain the alien pulls the knife out. Right as the alien charges at him with the knife; Mic pulls out his pistol and blasts it twice in the chest. The alien stops and falls to his knees. Mic stands in front of him, puts the gun to his head and finishes him off execution style. He takes comfort against a tree feeling his ribs. He now has to take shallow breaths. He grabs his knife from the alien and looks to rejoin the action. He marches to the line of troops anxiously looking about for the aliens. They scan the field looking for signs or evidence of where they are. If you look hard enough and close enough you can pinpoint one, you can spot their outline. Being good at doing so just requires experience. Some men spot there target with ease while others struggle. A hail of gunfire erupts deep in the forest. Mic with his 9mm still drawn picks a handful off as he runs over twigs and branches and through dense brush to catch up with his platoon. He and the rest of the men zig zag through the forest knowing a still target is easier to kill. It is so loud in the forest that third platoon can hear the echo screams from both their fellow soldiers and the aliens. They rush to aid them; however they are five miles from the tree line. They move in as fast as they can. They switch the sensors on the surveillance droid to infrared. As they approach the battle they move into stealth defense formation and each member of the platoon is relayed the coordinates of grouped aliens. They charge the fight and bring overwhelming fire power in favor of the soldiers within minutes the aliens are gunned down. The platoons take a few minutes to regroup and bring in Black Hawks for a dust off. Some soldiers collect souvenirs from the aliens. They continue their march north but after a few miles decide to rest and set up camp. They go to sleep with full stomachs and visions of the battle at Devils Den State Park will forever be imbedded in their minds.

Tomorrow brings a new day and it is a very important day for Jose and his crew. They have continued their reign in the sky as far as Pennsylvania and are ready to deploy from Philadelphia. Right away on their embark from left, right, and center they blast several space ships out the sky. More and more lay in pieces around the Comcast Sky Tower and scattered east spilling into the Atlantic. The fighting is fiercest here. A huge number of aliens populate the sky. They are countered by American forces. The most advanced stealth Black Hawks defend the shallow skies. Between them and the Stratus Guard they can advance to the mid Atlantic and prepare to take on the mother ship. Jose and his crew have maintained an impressive reputation and earned the nickname Sky Knights. After hearing this a young member of the Stratus Guard is anxious to earn his stripes and wants who he admires to admire him. His name is Edgar and like Jose who came out of the slums of St. Louis; Edgar came out the slums of Cleveland. He desperately wants to earn the right to fly side by side with Jose and his crew when they take on the mother ship. To get to that point they all will need to kill many aliens.

Edgar leads his platoon to flight. Right away he is side swiped by a smoking space ship. There is only minimal damage to the exterior of his air craft. He then sees three in a triangle shape up ahead. He goes for the one on his left first. He fires a few lasers, he nails his target. The other two return fire. He is hit, and one of his engines is badly damaged he knows in a little bit he will be down and engine. He banks left and tries to come at them from the side. With the engine failing he has limited mobility and can't bank as hard as he wants. He tries an up-down stutter approach. He misses with his first wave of lasers but the space ship flew upward right into his second wave. Then he circles around trying to take out the third one he was faced with. His engine has now completely failed. He flies head on towards his enemy. The alien fires first. Edgar sends his air craft into a spiral dodging the lasers beaming in at him. While in a spiral he rapid fires all his lasers blasting his opponent to pieces. He continues his air assault raid as he digs for the channel Jose is on. Jose pulls out some nifty moves of his own. He sings along to Metallica's "Unforgiven" as he swoops and splits opponents setting them ablaze mid air. Edgar reaches Jose on the radio,

"Jose you need to fly as an extension to me and my platoon, we all would be honored to have the Sky Knights fly with us taken on the mother ship."

"Who's this?"

"An aspiring Knight . . ." Only hearing their nickname a couple times he knows who he is talking to has been in the thick of things.

"I'm young I don't have the experience you got, but my talent rivals yours."

"Is that so, no one can match my greatness." He replies chuckling.

"Hey not your greatness but your skills as a flyer and shooter. I'm touching down on the coast we can swap stories over chow."

While on the ground Jose catches up with Edgar. He tells him all about where he is from, and how he grew up. Jose agrees he and his crew will fly up together to take on the mother ship. However Edgar needs new equipment if he is going to go up again. Later that night he receives an upgraded air mobile. This one is equipped with a fifth lasers mounted in the center. Jose goes with Edgar to receive the brand new stud craft, and to congratulate him on deserving it. Overwhelmed from Jose's confound enthusiasm Edgar suggests that Jose should get his air craft. Jose humbly declines.

"Muchas gracias Edgar maybe after mine has seen a few more years I'll receive one."

"You have already seen too many years!"

They both walk off to their respected bunks for the evening.

That night in northern Arkansas Mic and his battle buddy finish putting up their tent for the night. Mic aligns his weapons on his cot to clean each one. As he starts with his 9mm he also starts conversation with battle buddy.

"What's that you got?"

"What this?" Mic nods. "A mini hologram. My wife has the receiver I'm about to talk to her now." Mic continues his weapon cleaning. He admires the image as he cleans his M110. "You want to come over and say high?" Staff Sergeant Stephenson asks.

"Yea when I'm done cleaning this." Mic sets his weapon down and walks over. "What's your wife's name."

"Mary, just lean into the leans."

"Hi Mary nice to meet you."

"Mary this Sergeant Major Mic Von Haus."

"Sergeant Major, you don't have your own sleeping corridor?"

"No mam I move up in ranks not command. Where are you joining us from?"

"St Joseph Missouri. It's almost an hour north of Kansas City; I'm at John's parent's house now that's where we are all staying till John comes home. Our house is in the next town over in Cameron."

"How many kids do you guys have?" Mary steps back from the lens revealing they have one on the way. "Oh my congratulations! Is this . . .

"This is our first!"

"Congrats do you guys know what it is yet?"

"It's a girl!"

"Any names decided yet?"

"Not yet, hopefully Jonathan can be home within two months so we can further collaborate."

"Yea I have three girls."

"How cute, what are their names?"

"My oldest is Erica, then Stacy and the youngest is Jasmine. We live about 100 miles north of St Joseph in Red Oak, Iowa."

"Johns oldest brother Jay is staying with us, and their six kids 3 boys and 3 girls. And his youngest sister Josephene, they have three boys and one girl."

"Wow that's a full house. Although I'm sure at times you guys are on edge its nice and comforting to have lots of people around."

"Yea it's a bigger plantation with all the doors and windows boarded up."

"That's how my wife and kids are living. Our house has the maximum number of bedrooms needed and our cellar is stocked up with meat, and food, and water. I'm sure John and I are on the venture home soon."

"Yea what's the plan of operation for tomorrow?"

"We start heading north east towards Chicago, luckily the sears tower hasn't sustained an attack yet. We are going to be on foot the whole way; clearing rural areas till we get there. Hopefully we hit St. Louis in nine or ten days then Chicago in nine or ten more. The plan is to aid the fight in St. Louis and hopefully be done and return home but if not head on to Chicago."

"Be safe tomorrow, and the entire time you guys are out there."

"Thanks for the best wishes you guys do the same, stay safe till it's all over. Nice meeting you Mary; john is an excellent soldier I'm sure he will be returning shortly."

"Thanks Mic nice meeting you too BYE!"

"Take care." John continues on his conversation with his wife. Mic walks back over to his bunk, he has his own way of communicating with his wife and kids.

He pulls out his android tablet from his front pocket, the number one app on it is face time he selects that and then gets out his tripod stand and before he can finish setting it up Debra has answered hers and Mic can hear her sweet voice as he sets it up. He leans back and says,

"Hey Debra." He tries to sound enthused but his voice is weak as his eyes well up with tears.

"Hey Mic!" She also has tears in her eyes. "I missed you very much; I keep sitting by the android waiting for you at any minute."

"Oh yea in my free time your all I think about, you and the girls. How's everyone doing?"

"Good, give me a kiss." Debra leans in with her lips puckered up. Mic leans in smooching the lens, virally kissing her. "How are you?"

"I'm great! I miss you and the girls so much. Are any of them still awake?"

"They all are I'll have them say hi." After a brief moment all the girls appear in the screen with debras head sticking out above all of them.

"Hi daddy!" All of them say at once.

"Hi girls, you all staying safe?"

"Yes."

"All protecting momma?"

"Yes."

After a brief moment he says good night and virally kisses each one individually. "It was good seeing you honey. Sleep well, love and miss you."

"Love you too! What do you have planned for tomorrow?"

"We move out late morning and go North East to St. Louis then if it's still heavy battling we go on to Chicago."

"Ok be safe love and miss you, good night."

"Love you to good night sweet heart."

After Mic finishes up cleaning his weapons and making sure he has everything ready to go in the morning he sits down on his bunk and Staff Sergeant Stephenson joins him sitting on the cushioned blow up chair on the floor. Mic takes a picture of his family from his wallet, hands it to Stephenson and says,

"Do you know why I'm a good soldier." He pauses for a second. "I love my life, and hate all the lazy, selfish, cruel people surrounding it. I often come across a deer starved in a trap set by people who are too lazy to be proactive in both the care for their crops and the care for the animal. One; they have traps that do minimal damage to the animal, but it still starves because they don't go out to release it. They have automatic sprinklers so and until they need to go out to harvest they let the deer suffer." John being in the same National Guard Company knows he can relate.

"I know talk about cruel I arrested this farmer who killed two ten year old boys for being on his property. He said he was within his rights, but I'm glad a Judge didn't see it that way. For kids she knew there was an alternative route, she knew they were just playing and yelling at them would have taught them a lesson. He got life in prison."

"Good. You would think one day would go by with nothing cruel happening, but until you get rid of all the selfish, hateful, lazy, and cruel people in the world there will be many worries. On top of that there's an alien invasion. But you know what I plan to do about that . . .

"What?"

"Kill them all!"

"Yea Brotha!"

They stay up swapping stories not even getting a chance to think about tomorrow before they go to bed. In the morning the camp is at ease. Everyone is calm and collected, they take their time getting breakfast before they stagger into formation and move through the meadows.

The same can be said for everyone at base spread up and down the coast. There's no immediate threat so troops and airman joke around during breakfast and as they do one last equipment check. Jose, his crew and Edgar pile on a heaping breakfast. Edgar being new to military life knows how important it is to eat when you can, you may not get another meal in all day. Jose is chowing down he is much accustomed to living from chow time to chow time. The crew has high spirits. Then an Airman First Class walks by and says,

"Enjoy your meals it might be your last."

Edgar gets all railed up. "HEY! Why the hell you say something like that?"

The young Airman just pretends he didn't hear him and keeps walking.

"HEY, PUNTO!"

"Don't worry about it he didn't mean anything by it."

"You saw the smirk on his face."

Jose shrugs. "You can't let that bother you, you have to stay focused. He's just young, look at him he has his strut on he's focused, he's confident. You need to focus that energy towards the aliens."

"Yea but he said that to us, he is just a hatter."

"Hey, just forget about it."

Then Senior Airman Vilick comes up.

"Briefing at 10 30 at company command post."

Jose looks at his watch. "That's in 12 minutes lets hurry."

At the briefing Company Commander Major Benson of the United States Air Force lays it down for them.

"Listen up, at 12 30 we deploy. That's in 2 hours . . . less than 2 hours. We want you to get your head on right. Take this time to gear up, think about your loved ones. In less than two hours we take on the mother ship." Jose tunes out for a minute he instantly thinks of his wife and sons. He is determined to just get home to them as soon as possible.

"She is hovering south of us. We are going to fly at her from every angle. She has over a thousand minions protecting her right now she is ready to deploy thousands more as needed. All Airmen east of Omaha are being called to leave their post their focus is not on the tower they swore to protect. Today they fly to the coast, fuel up, gear up and deploy as needed. I say again deploy as needed don't be the sorry SOB they replace."

Once again Jose gives his attention to his Company Commander.

"Every Navy carrier available is scattered no more than 100 miles from America's coast you can land when necessary to re fuel. You may circle around and land anywhere on the coast to refuel as you already know. This will be 100,000 against 200,000 two against one at any given time. Gentleman, be weary of the mother ship, besides her main laser she may host thousands of lasers we don't know about. Penetrate that bitch over and over it is not likely she will surrender legs up, we will need to rub her face into the ground. When she goes down let's hope she doesn't land her fat ass in our back yard. Hopefully she lands in the ocean or that big bitch can land in Europe for all we care, and they are hoping the same for us. But let fatty destroy those old ass buildings just don't celebrate publicly if she does. It will be over with that fat bitch face down in the ocean. Any questions?"

"When we destroy the mother ship will we get to collect souvenirs?"

"Yes make sure none survived then take what memorabilia you would like, if she crashes in the ocean, no. Just don't fight each other for the coolest piece of rubble. That took six minutes do what you need to get your head straight and get ready."

Jose takes his time heading back to his Stratus Ship. Once back he takes out his communication android and talks to his wife and sons with face time.

"Hi sweet heart I got some good news we are launching a massive attack on the mother ship."

His wife gasps. "You are?"

"Yea it's a big task but if we take her down it's all done."

"Oh wow then you get to come home?"

"Not right then; of course there will be some stragglers. Can I say hi to the boys?"

"Of course . . ." His wife says with tears in her eyes. "Let me get them."

"Ricky, Jorge, Pablo, Carlos I love you. I got a feeling I'm going to be home real soon."

"We love you papa." Replies Ricky. "Kick some butt and come home."

"I will sons. Love you. May the force be with you." He says with a smile.

Jorge says, "May the force be with you dad love you." Then Pablo and Carlos say good bye. Right after Jose starts crying but he instantly turns the tears into fire in his eyes. He thinks to himself, to keep my family safe.

Right before takeoff it is so quiet you can hear a pin drop. Some are nervous, some are anxious and some are downright scared. There may be a thin line between nervous and anxious, no exception in this case. Jose tunes his IRMP3 to his favorite 20th century classic rock channel the first song to play is "Snuff the Rooster" by Alice in Chains. The masses take flight. Jose and the rest of the Sky Knights depart alongside Edgar and his platoon. The Knights fly in migration formation with Jose at the end next to Edgar. As they reach higher and higher they are not met with oppositions; it is the calm before the storm. After a short journey they see the mother ship. It is a marvelous sight, like nothing they have seen before. Green and yellow luminance lights make her a glowing bright spectacle in a vast emptiness. They can only marvel for so long before her guards swarm in defense. She opens her hatch and rows and columns of space ships flood the sky. Knowing at minimum they will need to take out two a piece the men of the Stratus Guard hover and wait. As the enemies spill out they do their best to pick them off. However they fly to fast right out the gate many stratus ships are met head on by the hefty alien space ships. Undamaged by the meager stratus ships they fly through much of the first wave candidly. A handful of soldiers lightly penetrate her backside. This act brings about her unerring decision to unleash more minions from the other side. The soldiers try to hold lines all around her. As they just keep spewing more and more out into the open sky the stratus ships scatter, frantically maneuvering as quick and as fast as they can attempting to avoid collisions and being met with a hail of laser fire. Edgar and Jose have not lost sight of each other. Side by side they blast their share of space ships out of the sky. The loss of their own is being multiplied by the tens and growing. Every minute ground command is deploying waves of airmen. Within one hour the number of airmen has been cut in half. The companies west of Omaha will be called up to go against the mother ship in another hour unless the numbers start to sway in favor of the troops. As that moment approaches the best of the airmen up there is dwindling thin. Not only is their fuel running out but for some their electromagnetic radiation emissions are weakening.

In the pentagon the secretary of defense Four Star General Hawkins discusses further strategies with President Polk-Mason. With blueprints laid out General Hawkins suggests his plan.

"We are losing too many too fast Mr. President. From our launch positions in Nevada and up and down California we can launch our Mother of all Bomb

Missiles. We have her coordinates we could have direct hits from as many as 100 missiles. We wouldn't need that many so it would not be necessary to send that many, but if eight to ten would be sent at first."

"If those are detected?"

"She may get on the run but not likely no matter where she goes these missiles will fallow. If she attempts to interfere with space ship blockage lasers will reflect off the missiles and the space ships will need to meet the missiles head on. By the looks of things we will need to deploy those weapons in 45 minutes from now. Hopefully our airmen can continue to at minimal deliver the same number of damage to the vessel. Simply for the sake of launching these weapons; if the level of destruction greatly decreases there won't be any men up there keeping her busy while these missiles deploy. We will need to maintain secrecy to avoid being intercepted mid air . . . if so we would launch a second attack from California and Nevada and shortly after from Montana,

Wyoming, Colorado, and New Mexico. From there any and all launch sites may be activated."

"Hopefully the first set hit her. Give me details on keeping secrecy."

"We would not tell our Airmen to evacuate so not to rouse suspicion until the missiles are two minutes from impact. We would radio to ground command five minutes before impact."

"Let's do it."

"We will continue to monitor their progress and the decision to activate first round of launch will be minute to minute. From there it will be a second to second decision."

Mic and his platoon continue their embark towards the Anheuser Busch Tower. It is close to night time now; they have made it past Branson and are currently traveling along James River. They settle near a bank for chow. The men chow down on MRE's. Mic spots a Private sitting next to him.

"Hey Private when you're done take two other guys with you and fill up all three, three gallons from this river. Boil it roughly one gallon at a time. Have everyone top off their canteens. Hurry up because it will be dark in half an hour. We will set up camp after chow. Have Edwards and Rodgers start the fire, tell them not to big at first till we are done boiling the water. They can set up their tents after the fire is started, then you guys after everyone has filled their canteens."

After finishing his chow Mic makes sure he has drank his canteen dry. Mic has an eerie feeling about tonight. The entire campaign they have not encountered a night attack. He remembers hearing from the news the aliens can see very well at night. From all his military action Mic can see very well at night also and can counter their inferred vision with night vision goggles. While he and Stephenson set up their tent he stops for a second and digs through his rucksack to make sure he has his goggles handy. By the time they get their tent set up and settled in the water is done boiling. Mic and Stephenson allow others to finish up before they get theirs. They have not yet determined order of night guard duty yet but Mic grabs his 9mm and his knife. He can't shake the notion that they are being watched. He is right. He takes a seat around the bonfire. Not long after a startling, bone chilling massacre happens right next to him. Three soldiers standing by the fire; their stomachs seemed to burst open. It was aliens that had snuck up on them and pierced their tails right through their mid sections. Mic jumps up and draws his pistol. He sees half a dozen run into tents and rip apart his comrades. A hail of frantic gun fire erupts. Stephenson comes running out with his knife in hand and meets one mid stride digging his knife into its gut. At the last second Mic sees one slash at him with his tail Mic turns to run. The first direction he runs is towards the water. He doesn't stop he gets in above his knees and takes a dive. He swims downstream and looks back he can see the alien gaining on him he tries with all his might to swim faster and faster. In water the alien's claws retract and webbing around his fingers flares out. The efficiency of his flat spear head tail in the water helps him gain on Mic fast. He grabs a hold of Mic's ankle and tries pulling him back. Mic is desperate for air and kicks hard at the alien freeing himself and he is able to come up for air and then heads towards shallower water. Thanks to evolving to have gills the alien looks like a giant serpent under water stalking him. The alien swims right for Mic's feet knocking him up out of the water. Mic lands on his back brushing against the sand. The alien dives on top of him holding him under. Mic struggles to come back up. The force of the alien is too much. Fully submerged the alien brings itself close to Mic's face. Mic stares the alien in the black sol less eyes. The thought of giving up enters Mic's mind. Then he quickly reaches for his knife holstered around his thigh, pulls it out and stabs the right in his gills. The alien lets out a loud vicious yell. It puts its hand over its neck and stands over Mic. When Mic thrusts the knife in, it slipped and he lost grip. The knife drifts downstream. Mic stands toe to toe with the alien. The alien draws out his claws. Mic needs to act quickly; he dives past the alien. Before the alien can turn to dive after him mic turns towards land climbs out and quickly retreats back towards camp. At a flat out sprint he can out run the alien. He makes it to his tent. Everything in there is scattered. He scrambles for his M249 rifle. He grabs it; with it over his shoulder he peers out the tent opening. He can't see the alien. All he can see is a few lifeless bodies surrounding the fire. He runs towards the fire and grabs a long log sticking out. He knows that if he keeps his head on a swivel and the burning log out in front of him the alien will need to carefully pick it's time to strike. Just down the field a dozen men are huddled keeping eyes on any lurking. They spot one coming up on Mic; they can make out the outline. They shout to Mic,

"Behind you! Behind you!"

Mic swings around right away he can see it and lashes at it with his blazing branch. He hits it in the throat. He takes another swing. The alien catches it and jerks it out of his hands. Mic pulls up his weapon and holds down the trigger. He shoots it at least twelve times before releasing the trigger. He turns to join his friends. It would be a fool's paradise to celebrate this victory, half the platoon was killed. He who remains picks up what he can. They piece the puzzle back together minus some pieces and get a short night sleep. Before he hits the sack Mic calls in for aid and supply to come in the morning. He is told about the mother ship crash landing on the coast of Western Sahara. If he holds tight they will be picked up by Black Hawks and lifted to the Anheuser Busch Tower. He relays the information face to face to all his men and once again their spirits are lifted. All the platoons will be going to rid what is left of the enemy in that the area. All over thousands still on the ground and swarming the air will need to be obliterated.

Just before Mic's platoon was ambushed Jose and fellow airmen were in the fight of their lives. Jose is taking his first attempt at penetrating the mother ship.

He swoops in between a couple of safe guards and opens fire penetrating the mother ship but not very deep. Her wounds are to minuscule compared to the rate they're losing men. To dodge traffic Jose flies around her back side knowing he can do a lot of damage internally from there. Edgar ducks and dives traffic as well. Like driving the lane two on one Edgar picks which one he is going to take out first and does so as he splits the defenders then picks off the other. He lands five of five next to where Jose hit her. Edgar trails Jose taking the long route around.

President Polk-Mason and General Hawkins are monitoring the situation.

"We are losing too many." Says the president.

"We are going to have to launch. They are synchronized to hit in 15 minutes. We will send our notice to the troops in ten minutes."

The president on the phone gets connected to all the launch sites and gives the command to launch the missiles.

"We will radio to command in ten minutes."

Jose is trying to make his way safely to the back of the ship unaware Edgar is trailing him. They get the call from command.

Command: "you have three minutes to get 20 miles from the blast radius of MOB's."

"We got to fire on her from here."

"That's you behind me Edgar I almost didn't see you . . . there's too much traffic here, plus I can do more damage there."

"The MOB's will do that."

"What if they don't make it? Plus the MO is to take out as much as we can." Jose shoots two more space ships down.

"Alright."

"I'll be able to make it in plenty time."

Edgar banks after blasting the mother ship a number of times, retreats down and out. Jose flanks around lines up and blast it. He turns to run and is clipped by a space ship. He flys ok but he can't turn as hard and lost some speed. He has to cautiously take it down he is still in blast zone. He looks to his left, he sees a space ship flying beside him. He jerks it right but the turn is too hard to handle; his air craft stalls. He is free falling. He looks behind him the space ship is gone. He does not panic he gets a firm grip on the eject lever and waits for his moment to pull it. When he is low enough he gives it a tug. Nothing happens, he has a picture of his wife and boys on his dash he looks at them for a second and thinks, I love you guys and gives it another forceful tug. Again nothing happens. Frantically he jerks and pulls on the ejection lever. He starts banging on the roof trying to get it to fly off. He tries jerking the lever and hitting the roof. He looks forward; he can see the ocean closing in. He stares at his picture till he hits the water then all he sees is black. He is not capable of a final thought before his heart stops beating.

Edgar finds room on a fleet carrier in the mid Atlantic to land on. He leaps out his air craft with his fists held high. He looks around for his buddy Jose. When he does not see him he is not consumed by the notion he landed elsewhere further away but he is consumed by the notion that Jose died. Edgar lifts off his helmet revealing his face. He looks up to the sky as to say, I hope you get to see this. Then directs his attention to where the explosion is about to happen. With his chin held high a tear streams down his face right before the bright flash and giant fire ball consumes the night time sky. From where he is at it looks like a portion of the sun falling out of the sky.

Edgar heads home; when he enters he takes a long look around at everything in his apartment. It's not even filled with his fiancé but has an extreme amount of joy in it. All the objects that surround him in his home take a new meaning to him. Like being guided by this ultimate being force he sits down in his lounge chair and realizes he has a new perspective on life. He has this feeling like that force guiding him is always going to be there. He knows not to take the guiding for granted; he has never felt it before. He knows not to take anything for granted. Shortly after he sits down his fiancé comes in and the room seems even more vibrant and full of life. He smiles at her, it's a smile not forced, it's one he can't help because at that moment he knows exactly what he needs to do to fulfill his life.

In the morning Mic and his company hold steady till the supplies gets on its way. Then the company marches to the highway to get to the drop off and pick up point. Plans change once all of America finds out the mother ship was destroyed. To their surprise more strykers and humvees are there to take them into Illinois. Mic rides in a Humvee all the way to Springfield. They get the night off then they may need to go on patrol for a couple weeks before going home. They turn an old camp ground into base. After getting set up he talks with Sgt Stephenson.

"We skipped over protecting the Anhueser Busch Tower."

"I know." Says John.

"When the aliens got word the mother ship is down over half of them split. There is still a bunch who want to stick around and fight till the end."

"Did you hear the force fields are gone."

"No kidding!"

"And since the mother ship went down many civilian militia has formed ranks. We will probably see them fighting tomorrow when we go out."

"Yea I kind of hope we head all the way north to interstate 80."

"Yea you want to march that far."

"I figure why not; do clean up duty then I can make my way home down 80. You need to head that way too right?"

"Yep."

"I'm sure there will be a couple Strykers or Humvees taking us back to base."

The next day the whole company seems to be in a lifted synchronization. Everyone has elevated their game. After whipping out a pack in Petersburg night time falls and morning rises and once again they are on the move. Sure enough as they get further north they run into a militia tracking through the fields, making progress on pending kills. Mic and his platoon know where aliens are hiding out. They set positions to raid some old abandoned plantations. Just as they are getting there some aliens are escaping and are tracked by Mic and other snipers. They find them on the edge of a vast privately owned forest already gunned down by the owners. Mic and his Platoon gather on the highway and wait to be hauled back to base.

Once at base the platoon and others freshly back celebrate with laughter, cheers, and with beers and celebration stogies. For a couple of hours all that is on their mind is how good it feels to be alive. The celebration is short lived for so many are anxious to get home. While celebrating Mic, John and a couple others uncover an old army jeep. With a stogy in mouth Sgt Barnes says,

"I'm gona see if I can drive this sucker."

He starts it up puts it into gear and hits the gas although he expected it to go forward he slams on the breaks and the guys yell,

"You have to put it in drive numb nuts."

"Where is every one heading? I'm driving."

"Mic says head west about five miles you'll hit my house." He hops in the front seat. Sgt Jones says. "I'm five miles east."

"I'm with him but a few more miles west then about five miles south."

"Alright, you're first Jones, then you Mic."

"Alright."

They crack open a fresh beer and get on their way. Mic pulls out a freshly rolled victory stogy and they pass it around. A handful of troops fly over head on their way home; some firing off rounds in the air to empty their clips and as a way to say a job well done, stay safe. They pull up to Jones' house; his you can see from the old interstate.

"See ya Jones." They call out as he turns to head up his drive. They whip the jeep around and head in Mic's direction when they get to his street he tells Barnes this will be fine. He tells them it's just a mile down the road. He tells them just a mile when it's actually three because he wants to walk alone and finish his beer. Plus he wants to be by himself for a minute to gather his thoughts. The only thought on his mind is he's thrilled to be alive and he can't wait to see his family.

Chapter 6

THE AFTERMATH

Mic finishes the last swig of his beer a mile shy of his house. He holds on to the empty bottle till he gets home. He walks up his steps to his door he can't wait to go in. He sets his bottle off to the side and walks through his rigged up door way. With his gear strapped to his back the girls run up elated to see their father and give him a big hug as they call out "Daddy!"

"Hey girls, how are you ladies? I missed you."

"We missed you too Dad!"

"What are you up to?"

"Nothing." Says Jasmine.

"Playing fit games and watching TV." Says Stacy.

"Where's your momma?"

"In the yard." Says Jasmine as she points out back.

"Alright love you guys, you can get back to playing."

"Love you Dad."

Mic takes his pack off at the door and leans it against the wall. He walks out into the yard. Deb is digging some plots for the tomato plants, and has a bucket of warm water to help soften the ground. She hears some footsteps. She looks up and as soon as she sees who it is she yells, "Mic!" Then runs over and embraces him with a big hug. They have a long kiss hello. He puts his arm around her waist and walks her back into the house. Mic's eyes are welled up with tears and Deb has them streaming down her cheeks. They go inside and sit down in the kitchen. The girls turn off the monitor and anxiously walk over to their father eager to hear him talk about anything.

"I'm sure you guys knew the mother ship was destroyed."

"Yea!" They all say joyfully.

Deb says, "We slept almost every night in the bunker."

"I see the windows got boarded up, and what happened to the front door."

"An alien busted through." Momma explains. Mic raises his eyebrows. "last week I saw one coming towards our house, the girls ran down stairs and hid."

"Mom killed it in your guy's bedroom."

"Way to go Deb! Where is it?"

"The girls helped me drag it to the fire pit, and we poured gasoline on it and burned it."

"I was hoping you kept it or kept part of it. Like its tail or at least a claw."

"That's what Stacy said." Erica told him.

"Yea Stacy said we should keep a claw or cut off his hand and keep it."

"Were not butchers." Deb states.

"Yea at least we have a tail."

"Do you think we could get a lot of money for it?" Asks Erica.

"Yea, and a lot more money in thirty years or more. But I'm going to keep it forever."

"Yea we wouldn't sell it Erica." Says Jasmine.

"I know but I was thinking if it was ever worth over a million dollars or something."

"By the way we need to get it stored in ice, has it already rotted . . ."

Deb intervenes, "I put it in a bag and put it in the freezer already."

"Oh good, I didn't think of that at the time." He pauses, "I'm hungry."

"I can make you something."

"Um I'm hungry for a sandwich I'll make it."

Everyone gathers around their father and husband.

"As soon as I'm done eating I will take the boards down. Hey did you guys hear the force fields are gone."

"Yea they went down with the mother ship." Says Deb.

When Mic is done he skips over taking the boards down and goes straight to playing with his girls. Like taking down the Christmas tree he will get to it in a couple more weeks. He plays online games with them and streams television shows, and they read stories and relax on the couch together. He flips the monitor in the wall to window view. They talk about nature and listen to some history stories. Then in the evening Mic prepares dinner and when the family is done eating he shares various battle stories with his girls. His favorite about fighting the alien in the river is saved for last.

The next morning he emphasizes staying in bed. Deb debates telling him about Randy but decides not to tell him now. If she does tell him it will be later down the road. In retro spec it's just gossip and he may not care to know what happened; although she feels obligated to tell him the truth especially since she knows he will keep it to himself. She just doesn't want to put that on his mind right now. So she takes advantage of being in bed with Mic and locks lips with him.

"It's so nice to have the week off. What should we do?"

"I'm not sure." Replies Deb.

"Should we go camping or fishing . . . or both?"

"Yea let's go tomorrow."

"Ok we can come back Saturday evening. Where should we go? North to South Dakota or south to the Ozarks."

"I like the Ozarks . . . but we haven't gone to South Dakota in a long time."

"I could fly us to South Dakota in the extender and you could fallow with the supplies."

"Ok let's do that. Let's get some things done around here and then pack tonight."

They get their chores done and leave in the morning and in two hours they reach their destination. Luckily it hadn't snowed much in that portion of South Dakota and has warmed up just enough to enjoy being outside.

"It's great enjoying hot chocolate around the fire and enjoying s'mores."

"Yea, I'm glad we brought the arctic equipment."

"Me too, being cold though makes us sleep closer. Hey I'm going to see if I can catch fresh walleye for supper tonight."

"Take Jasmine with you she is itching to go."

"I will."

"What time do you want to leave tomorrow?"

"Three or four."

"Ok."

Mic and Jasmine catch one but it is smaller so they toss it back. Then Mic reels in a big one.

"Hey this will do for supper."

"Oh yea look how big he is." Jasmine says enthusiastically. She runs back to camp to tell everyone about the catch. "Dad was reeling in as fast as he could." She then proceeds to do her impression of her Poppa. The next day they round off the trip with playing catch with the Frisbee and the football, and then return home. When they get home the mailbox is filled to the brim. Mic opens the only thing addressed to him sent from his bases command post. He gives careful consideration to the content before sharing it with his wife. He tucks it away and decides either after breakfast or during lunch is the best time to share with her what command had to say.

"What's for lunch babe?" Asks Mic

"I'll go in and make us something." Replies Deb.

Once inside she gets supplies out to cut up some turkey meat and fresh fruit.

"Hey babe what do you think I should do in the near future?"

"What do you mean?"

"I'm going to get promoted to Command Sergeant Major. They want me in charge of the whole company."

"That's great!"

"Yea I think so too, but I sort of want to be home more often."

"What else were you thinking of doing?"

Mic shrugs. "I keep getting promoted because I keep raking up deployment hours. I won't have to worry about that being company commander. Well I'll still get deployed with the whole company, but no more individual platoon or squad deployment."

"And as commander you stay off the front lines and command from the rear."

"Yea, plus it seems we wouldn't get deployed again for a long time. Doesn't it feel like everyone is more unified . . . not just here but the whole world?"

"It certainly does."

"I would be the highest paid enlisted rank."

"What else were you thinking about doing."

"I could probably make even more money farming more along with professionally hunting. If we got a couple of cows and a bull; we could also raise a couple horses to sell. Plus providing food for people around here. I could charge per pound and depending on the type of animal; some rare delectable's could make me a lot of money. Two things though; now I would have to travel pretty far for anything I hunt but that would make the price go up which is good and bad.

"you could charge slightly less than other hunters."

"Yea and I know you could handle the extra chores in my absence . . . I could trust how you sell the horses. However there may be times where I'm gone for more than a couple days getting the meat desired."

"There is definitely pros and cons."

"Another option could be just going out once a month for however long. It would be a good change of pace for me. And my main focus would be keeping the balance on the farm. With our three and a half acres we could fit another half acre of corn and another half acre of wheat. That would be a sizeable contribution to our neighbors and our pocketbook."

"Think about it that would be profitable if we could harvest year round."

"I wasn't thinking it wouldn't make us a huge profit year round but that's where hunting would come in."

"Yea but would the money you make be worth the time your spending."

"You're right, but I still want to think about my options because I'm just not 100 percent sure it's what I want to do the rest of my life."

"You are so good at it though."

"I am great soldier."

"You would be leading other good soldiers. You would be showing them what you know. Commanding them with your knowledge and skill; you could ratify a more proficient front line fighting."

"I think so too. I love you honey."

A couple of weeks go by and the family continues on with their routine. The girls continue their lessons with their teacher. Mic has gone hunting with his bow and arrow. He kills only what his family requires. In three days he takes home a coyote, a bobcat and a deer. Spring time is officially here and with summer approaching the world wide unity maintains. As everyone knows keeping ones sanity throughout winter keeping ones sanity is key. Things always look up once the weather is nice. Once summer time comes Mic and the family take another vacation. This time to a more exotic location. Mic takes them to California and they sail to Hawaii.

"We haven't done our share of procreating Mic. Let's have the girls stay in the room and we should get a private cabana on the beach."

"I like our hypocritical approach to procreating."

"What about one more."

"Tell you what I will think about it in the cabana. Let's go!"

The cabana is very calming and relaxing. The floor has a layer of daffodil and purple tulip flower peddles. There is only room for a TV, a mini bar and a bed. The close corners make it very intimate. The speakers mounted in the corners produce very relaxing traditional Hawaiian music. The music is just soft enough to still hear the waves rushing up the shore. The aroma candles are another reminder of the far away paradise that the whole island provides.

"I love it in here it's very provocative." Mic states.

Deb rolls over on the bed face down. Mic massages her back with scented oils.

"I could stay here forever." Says Deb.

"This is where I could retire and cook shrimp almost every day."

"Let's retire today."

Mic kisses Deb right between the shoulder blades. He kisses her again lower on her back. With his hands he pulls down her shorts a little bit and kisses the small of her back. Then he grabs her shorts at the legs and yanks them down to her knees. She provides help by lifting her legs up so he can slide them off. He grips her ass firm with both hands. He then slides her laced black thong off. She turns over and takes her top off. Mic copies her. He leans forward and with his tongue starts at her earlobe and makes his way down her neck to her collar bone. She lets out a passionate moan. She reaches her finger tips into the waist of his shorts. Mic gives her a passionate kiss then lays on his back. Deb glides her tongue over his nipples. While she gives them a lick she undoes his shorts then pulls them off. After making love they lie on the bed quietly reflecting on life in general. Then they enjoy the rest of their vacation with their beloved girls. They don't know it yet but they return home with one more on the way.

About the Author

Matt Rittenhouse is a husband to one loving mother and father to four loving daughters. His four daughters provide a great deal of inspiration to his book. The character Mic, although fictional reflects his personal morals and principals. He was born and raised in Cedar Rapids, Iowa. Having traveled from coast to coast and including the gulf coast he is familiar with various parts of the country and is accustom to the destinations Mic travels to on his journey. As Matt's journey continues he plans on having his beautiful wife and girls accompany him to all the magnificent places this world has to offer. For him it's all about how he gets to his destination and making sure he soaks it all in once he arrives. His goals in life are to make sure he gets the most out of every adventure in his path and to never stop looking for a new one. Matt enjoys the simple pleasures and has a strong desire to do what he loves. His passion for life spews out on the pages of his book They Came, We Conquered. It is his first novel and hopefully it ignites the bright burning light to a long and prosperous career in novel writing. Hope you enjoy reading it even more so than he did writing it.